NORTH DOME

TENAYA CANYON

HALF DOME

Tenaya Creek

GLACIER POINT

N

THE
WOLF
KEEPERS

ELISE BROACH

WITH ILLUSTRATIONS BY
ALICE RATTERREE

Christy Ottaviano Books

Henry Holt and Company | New York

Henry Holt and Company
Publishers since 1866
175 Fifth Avenue
New York, New York 10010
mackids.com

Library of Congress Cataloging-in-Publication Data
Names: Broach, Elise, author. | Ratterree, Alice, illustrator.
Title: The wolf keepers / Elise Broach ; with illustrations by
    Alice Ratterree.
Description: First edition. | New York : Henry Holt and Company, 2016. |
    Christy Ottaviano Books. | Summary: Twelve-year-old Lizzie Durango
    lives in a zoo, spending her days taking note of the animals' behaviors,
    then she meets runaway Tyler Briggs and together they investigate the
    wolves who are suddenly dying.
Identifiers: LCCN 2015049899 | ISBN 9780805098990 (hardback)
Subjects: | CYAC: Zoos—Fiction. | Wolves—Fiction. | Runaways—
    Fiction. | Friendship—Fiction. | Mystery and detective stories. |
    BISAC: JUVENILE FICTION / Mysteries & Detective Stories. |
    JUVENILE FICTION / Social Issues / Friendship. | JUVENILE
    FICTION / Family / General (see also headings under Social Issues). |
    JUVENILE FICTION / Animals / Zoos.
Classification: LCC PZ7.B78083 Wo 2016 | DDC [Fic]—dc23
LC record available at https://lccn.loc.gov/2015049899

Our books may be purchased in bulk for promotional, educational, or
business use. Please contact your local bookseller or the Macmillan
Corporate and Premium Sales Department at (800) 221-7945 ext. 5442
or by e-mail at MacmillanSpecialMarkets@macmillan.com.

Book design by Liz Dresner

First Edition—2016

Printed in the United States of America by
R. R. Donnelly & Sons Company, Harrisonburg, Virginia

10 9 8 7 6 5 4 3 2 1

For my aunt and godmother,
Annette Lomont, who worked at the San Francisco Zoo
for many years and introduced me to all its wonders

ALSO BY ELISE BROACH

THE MASTERPIECE ADVENTURE SERIES
The Miniature World of Marvin & James
James to the Rescue

THE SUPERSTITION MOUNTAIN SERIES
Missing on Superstition Mountain
Treasure on Superstition Mountain
Revenge of Superstition Mountain

Masterpiece

Shakespeare's Secret

Desert Crossing

THE WOLF KEEPERS

I only went out for a walk and finally concluded to stay out till sundown, for going out, I found, was really going in.

—*John Muir*

WILD

A FEW FEET away, the wolf stared at Lizzie with pale silver eyes, ears pricking forward in sharp triangles. He stood perfectly still. In the space between them, she could feel a ripple of energy—a tension in the air like a string pulled taut. She imagined coming face-to-face with him in the woods, nothing between them. Despite the July heat, she shivered.

She was sitting on a rock between the low wooden guardrail and the chain-link fence: closer than the public was allowed, but Lizzie wasn't the public. Her father was the head zookeeper at the John Muir Wildlife Park in Lodisto, California, and Lizzie had lived there all her life.

The wolves, though—they were new.

They had come from a city zoo in the north, seven of them, and this was the big male, Lobo. It was one of the zoo traditions, giving the animals foreign-sounding names; in this case, Lobo, Spanish for wolf. Did Spain even have wolves? Lizzie didn't know, but maybe the Spanish explorers had encountered them in California centuries ago. There was something ancient about the wolves, as if they'd been around since the beginning of time, and nothing was likely to surprise or confound them.

"Hey, Lobo," she said softly. "Hey."

The wolf stared at her, his face alert.

She balanced her green spiral notebook on her knee-caps, and, opposite her sketch of Lobo, she wrote:

July 26. Wolf Woods. Lobo looks at me with the clearest, most pure silver eyes. What is he thinking? He doesn't seem afraid. I wonder if he sees me as a strange kind of animal, one without fur. Or maybe he just sees me as meat. If the fence weren't here, would he try to eat me?

She shuddered again. Was it possible the wolf thought she was prey?

"LOBO"
WOLF WOODS

Lizzie D.
7/26

CANIS LUPIS
(The gray wolf)

While most of the zoo animals had been bred in captivity, never actually experiencing the wild places that would have been their natural habitats, the wolves were different. These seven had been separately captured and rehabilitated, some injured by hunters or vehicles, some posing a threat to livestock. They had all come from the wild, and here at the zoo, they formed a pack.

For the past month, Lizzie had spent part of almost every day sitting at the edge of their enclosure, watching them. The John Muir Wildlife Park had never had wolves before, and the new exhibit, Wolf Woods, was the largest animal habitat at the zoo—almost two acres of scrubby meadow mixed with pine trees. It was so big that sometimes you couldn't even see the wolves. They would gather under the trees in the far corner, and for the impatient visitors who thronged into the viewing hut, the pen might as well have been empty. In fact, Lizzie's father had told her that the public had complained about this, disgruntled that the zoo's exciting new addition had turned out to be a bunch of animals who were determined to keep to themselves.

Privately, Lizzie thought all the zoo animals would do that, if given the chance. Why would they want to be near humans, with their bright clothes and strange smells and loud laughter . . . the assault of noisy, clumsy human habits? Lizzie was pretty sure that she, too, would prefer the back of the enclosure, in the shadows with the wolves.

Nearby, a child screeched with delight, and Lobo's ears flattened against his head. He backed away from the fence.

"Shhhh, it's okay," Lizzie murmured.

She shut the notebook and slid her pen through the metal spiral. Her summer homework assignment before the start of seventh grade was to keep a nature journal, in the tradition of John Muir, the great naturalist who was the zoo's namesake. This project had been the brainchild of the sixth-grade Language Arts team. Lizzie's teacher, Mrs. Yuan, told the students the teachers wanted to inspire three things: better writing, an interest in John Muir, and an appreciation of the scenic mountain landscape that was their home. The journal wouldn't be graded and the students could write in whatever style they liked, as long as each journal entry offered a personal reflection on some aspect of nature. But summer homework? To Lizzie, it sounded like a perverse violation of everything sacred about the summer, the long, lazy freedom of it, the way it existed outside the bounds of school time. Also, while she loved to read, she didn't much like writing. She had so many thoughts, and it was hard to pin them down adequately with words.

But keeping a journal for the past month had surprised her. First of all, she discovered that without the threat of a teacher reading and grading her writing, she actually *did* like to write. Writing in the notebook was like having a small, private conversation with the page: talking to herself, but on paper. The spelling didn't matter, the grammar didn't matter . . . only the ideas. Second, after a few weeks of regular writing, she found she had a notebook that was half full, and it seemed somehow substantial—all of her passing thoughts and comments, about the wolves, life at the zoo, plants and animals she'd looked at, recorded where she could read them and ponder them again and again. And finally, the very act of writing stuff down somehow changed the way she thought about things. Would it even have occurred to her that Lobo saw her as meat, if she hadn't been writing about him?

At least the students weren't expected to write like John Muir, who had a very flowery and lofty style, in Lizzie's opinion. They'd had to read excerpts from his journal, *My First Summer in the Sierra,* and some of his other writings, and Lizzie thought his words sounded like a sermon from church. She had copied some of his quotations in the front of her notebook, including: *"In God's wildness lies the hope of the world,"* and *"Between every two pine trees there is a door leading to a new way of life."* They were interesting, but also so abstract that it was hard to know what he really meant.

As Lizzie's Grandma May would say, John Muir was an odd duck. Lizzie had learned several strange facts about him: He was born in Scotland; he had memorized almost the entire Bible by the time he was eleven; after he came to America, he worked at a wagon wheel factory and a tool poked him in the eye, nearly blinding him; and a few years later, he walked all the way from Indiana to Florida, a distance of a thousand miles. John Muir had spent his entire life exploring the wilderness and fighting to keep it safe. And oh my goodness, how he liked to write! He had written page after page, letters, journals, and essays, and drawn sketches, too—enough to fill many published books—showing his love of nature: in particular, the Sierra Nevada mountain range that rose majestically just a few dozen miles from Lodisto.

And now John Muir was the reason Lizzie was keeping a journal all summer, one that was mostly about the wolves. Every day she came to Wolf Woods to watch them and write about what they were doing . . . stretching, playing, napping, squabbling. By now she felt like she knew them, especially Lobo. He was so used to her presence that he would walk over to the fence as soon as she appeared. The big wolf had a seriousness that intrigued Lizzie. He looked directly at her, in a way that was neither aggressive nor fearful. She knew that staring back at any animal in the dog family was considered a challenge; in the wild, it could provoke an attack. On the other hand, refusing to make eye contact signaled weakness and submission.

So she chose a middle ground, looking at the wolf, then glancing away. The wolf took a step toward her, sniffing the air. His shoulders were massive, and the thick halo of silvery fur made him seem even bigger. He looked nothing like a dog to Lizzie. There was something tightly wound in him, some wildness that was barely contained. She wondered what would happen if that ever broke through.

The rest of the pack clustered in the shade of the scraggly pines. Lizzie was worried about one of them, a brownish-gray female named Athena who seemed like she might be sick. She had thrown up earlier, and now she was lying on her side. Even at a distance, Lizzie could see her legs trembling.

"Little girl," an older woman in an orange blouse called to Lizzie from the sidewalk. "You should get away from there. You're too close."

Lizzie shifted slightly on her rock. "It's okay," she said politely. "My dad works here."

The woman looked disapproving, but she was forced to turn her attention to two small boys who were racing around the viewing hut, brandishing hot dogs as if they were swords. Probably her grandchildren, Lizzie thought.

"Jared, stop that," the woman scolded. "Ian! You're going to drop it. And I am not buying you another one."

Lizzie flipped open her notebook again and wrote, *Sometimes the people at the zoo seem wilder than the animals. The animals are so quiet, but the people are loud and agitated.*

She liked the word *agitated*. Her father used it to describe animals that paced nervously, unable to calm down.

The woman chased after the two boys, her voice rising. "Do you hear me? I am NOT BUYING YOU ANOTHER ONE."

Lizzie waited for one of the hot dogs to fall to the ground, since an adult's warnings so often seemed to guarantee the very disaster they were trying to prevent. But before that could happen, the woman grabbed each boy by the shoulder and herded them down the path toward the prairie dog exhibit, still lecturing.

 9

When Lizzie turned back to Lobo, she saw that he had retreated to the back of the pen. He was standing over the wolf on the ground, sniffing her nose. None of the pack had really settled into their new surroundings, but Athena had seemed the most anxious of any of them. And now she'd gotten sick. Lizzie sighed, closing the notebook again. There was no point in waiting. She knew the big wolf wouldn't come back to the fence. One thing she had learned from watching Lobo: He never changed his mind.

She tucked her feet beneath her and sprang up, suddenly hungry. One of the many great things about living at the zoo was that she could get a meal at the snack bar anytime she wanted, for free. Maybe a slice of pizza today, with a frozen lemonade. She hoped there wouldn't be a long line. She walked down the path, past the sprawling concrete building that housed the tropical rain forest, then past the vertical cage that held the bald eagle. He'd been rescued from the wild years ago, badly injured, with only one eye. Lizzie thought it gave him a rakish, pirate-y look. Then she took a shortcut behind the Barnyard, a farm-like setting that housed the petting zoo. Here, you could pet and feed the animals. The comical little goats rushed over to the fence when they saw her, and she scratched one between his curved horns.

When she reached the food court, it was almost noon, and the concrete plaza was crowded with families. Children ran around the tables, screaming and laughing. Harried parents balanced trays laden with the zoo's various fast-food offerings: slices of pizza, steaming hot dogs, onion rings, cups of swirly ice cream. Lizzie hugged her notebook to her chest and was just heading toward the end of the line when a skinny boy who looked about her own age cut in front of her.

Startled, she stepped back to make room for him, but she wasn't sure he'd even seen her. He had brown skin and hair that formed a cap of tight black curls. His shoulder blades made sharp lines through his blue T-shirt. He was watching the activity at a nearby table, where a mother was trying to corral several toddlers.

"No, Ben, this is your hamburger: The other one is for Noah," the mother chided. "Lily, hold my hand. Let's go get our drinks."

The woman pushed two trays of food into the center of the table and was guiding the three children toward the soda machine with a stack of empty cups when the boy, who had been standing quietly in front of Lizzie, suddenly darted out of the line and snatched one of the trays. Holding it in front of him, he strode quickly and purposefully across the plaza.

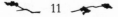

Lizzie was so surprised that she could only stare. Had he really just taken that family's lunch? He'd done it so boldly, she thought she must be mistaken.

One of the children—probably the one whose hamburger was moving swiftly across the plaza—began to wail. The mother, juggling cups and filling them in the foamy stream from the soda dispenser, swung around.

Lizzie hesitated for only a second. Dropping her notebook on an empty table, she ran after the boy.

Chapter 2

"YOU STOLE THAT!"

"HEY," SHE YELLED, dodging bodies in the crowded plaza.

The boy didn't slow down; if anything, he seemed to walk faster. Lizzie raced across the concrete, finally overtaking him. She grabbed his arm.

The boy whipped around and nearly dropped the tray. His dark eyes flashed as he scowled at her.

"What are you doing?" Lizzie demanded. "You can't take that."

"Let go," the boy warned.

They glared at each other over the red plastic basket heaped with french fries. Lizzie thought he looked familiar. There were some Lodisto families with zoo memberships who came to the zoo every week all summer long; maybe he was one of those.

"You stole that!" she said. "From a little kid." She grabbed one side of the tray and yanked.

The boy tightened his grip on the other. "Mind your own business," he hissed.

Then his expression changed, and he released the tray. As suddenly as he had appeared, he fled across the plaza, his blue shirt dappled by the sun.

"Give me that!" The mother of the children appeared at Lizzie's elbow, flushed and furious. "How dare you? I'm going to call security." She snatched the tray.

Lizzie started to explain that the boy was the one who'd taken their food, but something stopped her. She could still see his retreating back, shoulder blades poking sharply through his T-shirt. He was running up the path toward the elephant house.

She bit her lip, glancing from the fleeing boy to the enraged woman right in front of her.

"Sorry," she mumbled, looking at the ground. "I picked it up by mistake."

"By mistake? By *mistake*?" The woman leaned toward her, so angry she was spitting with every word, and Lizzie's heart jumped in her chest. "You stole that! My son's lunch! He's three years old—what is wrong with you, taking food from a little boy!"

Lizzie raised her eyes and looked at the woman. She tried to speak more firmly. "It was just a misunderstanding."

"That's ridiculous—" the woman exploded.

But then Lizzie felt a hand drop heavily onto her shoulder. Wesley Mack, one of the zoo custodians, was standing next to her.

"Is there a problem?" he asked the woman.

"Yes! Yes, there is." The woman glanced back at the three children, who were watching the scene with wide eyes. Even the one who had been crying seemed utterly mesmerized by his mother's outburst.

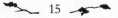

"This girl stole my son's hamburger! She took the tray right off our table."

Wesley Mack snorted. "I'm sure you're wrong about that. This is Lizzie Durango, the daughter of our head zookeeper, Mike Durango."

Lizzie could see the woman's posture change. A flicker of confusion crossed her face. "But—" she spluttered.

"Everyone here knows Lizzie," he continued. "And she can get whatever she wants from the snack bar. Doesn't cost her a dime. So there'd be no reason for her to steal your food."

"She took the tray! I had to run after her," the woman protested. But she took a step backward, her eyes flitting over to the three children.

Lizzie could tell that her fury was fizzling. It was like watching one of the wolves back down from a confrontation. . . . The aggression seemed to leak away. Was it because she believed Wesley? Or because he was bigger, a man, someone who worked at the zoo? Dominance—that's what her dad would say.

"You'd better get back to your kids," Wesley said.

The woman gripped the tray, staring at both of them. "You should be more careful," she said to Lizzie. Abruptly, she huffed back to her table.

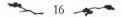

Lizzie tried to still her pounding heart. Something about being yelled at by a stranger was so unsettling—the unexpected intimacy of it, feeling that strong emotion coming from somebody you didn't even know. It felt like a violation.

"Thanks, Wesley," she said. "I didn't—"

"Of course you didn't." He brushed it off. "Tourists! They act like they own the place."

It was true that Lodisto was the last pit stop for tourists heading to Yosemite National Park, and as a result, the little town and its zoo drew lots of people from out of state: families who'd been sightseeing in San Francisco or LA and were looking to break up the long drive with a distraction for their kids. These visitors were often decked out in T-shirts or hats emblazoned with California themes—I LEFT MY HEART IN SAN FRANCISCO, or CALIFORNIA DREAMIN'—and they seemed both excitable and vaguely bored, so that the smallest event could trigger outsized reactions.

"They're crazy," Wesley continued dismissively.

"Yeah," Lizzie agreed.

But she knew full well that there was nothing crazy about the woman's reaction. Someone *had* stolen her son's lunch.

She scanned the plaza. There was no sign of the boy.

Chapter 3

NOBODY

LIZZIE WALKED WITH Wesley back to the food line, which now snaked around the plaza, twice as long as before. She reclaimed her notebook from the table where she'd dropped it.

"Still writing in that notebook?" Wesley asked her.

Lizzie nodded.

"Want to read me something?"

She shook her head, feeling shy. "It's private."

"That so?" He had a teasing look on his face, but when she clutched the journal protectively against her chest, he relented. "What do you want for lunch? I'll go in the back and get us something."

Lizzie smiled at him. She loved Wesley. Even though he had no kids of his own, he had certain unassailable beliefs about being a kid: that you had the right to climb any wall or fence that presented itself; that anytime you dropped your ice cream, you got another one, no questions asked; and that you should never, ever have to wait in line.

"Cheese pizza, please," Lizzie said. "And a frozen lemonade."

"You got it."

Wesley walked around the side of the snack bar, while Lizzie waited under an oleander tree, shaded by its spiky leaves and pink blossoms. She thought about the boy and felt piqued. First of all, it was horrible to be screamed at, by a stranger no less, for something you didn't do. It made her feel sick to her stomach, and that was his fault, because he'd run off and left her to take the blame. (Okay, maybe that wasn't quite fair, because she could have told the woman the boy stole the food. The little kids would have backed her up . . . if they could even talk. But she hadn't wanted to tattle on him. She didn't know why.)

Second of all, even though the zoo was full of tourists, it wasn't a spot where people did things like that. There weren't muggings. There weren't fistfights. It wasn't

a place where people committed crimes. Sure, they broke the rules . . . They tapped on the glass of the exhibits in the rain forest, or they threw food to the animals, or they wandered into areas that were off-limits. Her father complained about these infractions, as did Wesley and the rest of the zoo staff. But it was generally accepted that zoo visitors didn't mean any harm. They were just excited and careless and ignorant. They were on vacation in a place full of animals they'd never seen before. They didn't always think about what would happen if, say, you threw part of your hot dog over the wall into the giraffe compound. Lizzie knew that giraffes were herbivores, which meant they didn't eat meat. So eating a hot dog might make them sick—and because their necks were very long, giraffes couldn't easily throw up, like, for instance, a hyena could.

So while zoo visitors did make mistakes and cause problems, they generally didn't do it on purpose. But the boy? There seemed to be no question that he'd meant to steal the food. Not only that, it seemed clear to Lizzie that it was something he'd done before. He had waited until the exact moment when the mother left the table, and when he took the tray, he walked quickly but didn't run . . . probably to avoid attracting attention.

Why would he steal food? The only reason Lizzie could think of was that he was hungry and had no money. But where were his parents or friends? Kids never came to the zoo alone.

And now here she was, with the food court more crowded than ever, having to wait for her lunch—if not in line—all because of that dumb boy. It made her mad. And he hadn't even seemed grateful when she took the blame for him! He'd just run off. If she saw him again, she would have a few things to say to him, she decided.

"Here you go," Wesley said, reappearing with a paper plate that sagged under the weight of two pizza slices. "And here's your lemonade." He handed her a jumbo-size cup frosted with condensation.

"Thanks, Wesley." Lizzie beamed at him. "You're the best."

"I sure am," he agreed, hoisting his own plate of food over his head like a waiter. "Back to work!"

Lizzie grabbed a napkin and straw and carried her lunch up the path toward the elephant house. She was looking for a blue shirt.

At the elephant house, the two elephants, Timbo and Belle, stood flank to flank in the dusty yard, their tails swishing. Belle's long trunk stretched up into a nearby tree and curled over a thin, leafy branch, tugging until it broke loose. Pinching it with the end of her trunk, she swung it over Timbo's back and scratched his neck with it. His big ears flapped appreciatively. The elephants were some of the smartest animals at the zoo, according to Lizzie's father.

With her notebook clapped under one arm, Lizzie cradled the pizza in the greasy paper plate and took small bites from the tip. It was molten with cheese and blisteringly hot, so she followed each bite with a sip of the sweet, tart, slushy lemonade, cold enough to numb her tongue. There was still no sign of the boy.

She walked along the curve of the path toward the giraffes, with their impossibly long necks and their beautiful, soft eyes. One of the most amazing things Lizzie had ever seen at the zoo was a baby giraffe being born. The mother gave birth standing up, and the baby had tumbled through the air, falling more than five feet and landing in a jumble of knobby limbs on the straw.

But the baby hadn't been hurt at all. Moments later, after the mother finished licking it with her long, black tongue, the baby had wobbled to its feet and stared right at Lizzie with huge eyes, blinking its long lashes.

There was no sign of the boy by the giraffe enclosure. Lizzie glanced up the hill, toward the tiger cage. This was the part of the zoo she hated—a line of old cages that hadn't been replaced yet. Most of the other exhibits at least tried to mimic the animals' natural environments, but these just looked like prison cells. Lizzie had heard all the arguments from her father about how the zoo's mission was conservation and education; how virtually all zoo animals were born in zoos, so they didn't "miss" the wild; how so many of these animals would face extinction if there weren't zoos to create safe, healthy places for them to breed and survive. But her father hated this old section of the zoo as much as she did, and it was his top priority to raise enough money to replace it with larger, more natural-looking habitats.

The Siberian tiger paced back and forth, back and forth, along the perimeter of his cage. The hopelessness of it made Lizzie cringe.

Then she saw the boy.

He was sitting on the low curb in front of the tiger exhibit, watching the tiger, his back facing Lizzie.

She walked slowly toward him, thinking if he heard her, he might run.

When she was a few feet away, she said, "Hey."

The boy jumped up, spinning around. He glared at her. "What do you want?"

Lizzie frowned at him. "You could say thank you."

"For what?" he demanded. "Taking my food?"

"It wasn't your food! You stole it."

The boy scanned the walkway, quick, darting looks that seemed full of nervousness and guilt.

"I didn't steal nothing," he said.

"You did too! I saw you."

"I did not. They were finished! They left it on the table."

Lizzie shook her head at him in disbelief. "The mom was taking the kids to get drinks. You grabbed their lunch before they even had a chance to sit down."

A flicker of doubt crossed the boy's face. He seemed about to argue with her further, then abruptly changed his mind. "It's not like those little kids were gonna eat it. She bought way too much."

That was probably right, Lizzie thought. There had been a lot of food on the table, and little kids never ate much of their lunch, in her experience. They were usually more interested in playing with it.

"It doesn't matter. She paid for it," Lizzie said. "You can't take it just because you think there's too much for them to eat."

He shrugged. "Well, I thought they were finished. People leave food on the tables all the time."

"I had to give it back," Lizzie protested. "And then that woman blamed *me*."

The boy's dark eyes widened, and for the first time, he looked worried. "Did you get in trouble?"

Lizzie hesitated. She wanted him to feel bad, but not *that* bad. Maybe he really had thought the family was finished with their meal. "The mom yelled at me," she told him, "but it ended up okay."

The boy relaxed. "See? It would have been a lot worse for me."

Lizzie looked away, embarrassed. She suspected he was right.

But the boy seemed suddenly cheerful. He pointed at her plate, greasy and curling under its one remaining slice of pizza. "You eating that?"

"I'm not hungry," she said, thrusting the plate at him. "Do you want it?"

The boy didn't wait. He seized the plate and

plopped back down on the curb, folding the pizza in half and shoving it into his mouth. When he was almost finished with it, he paused. He rolled the crust inside the paper plate and crammed it into his shorts pocket.

Lizzie had never seen a person eat like that. He had gulped it down frantically, but he was clearly saving some for later.

Mesmerized, she held out her lemonade.

"You done with that, too?" he asked, snapping off the lid and guzzling it. It splattered over his shirt. A moment later, the cup was empty.

"Wow," Lizzie said.

He wiped his mouth on his arm. "What?"

"Nothing," she said quickly. "I guess you were hungry."

"So?" He crunched the empty cup with his foot.

She shrugged. "Nothing," she said again, still watching him. "I'm Lizzie Durango," she said. "I live here. My dad's the head zookeeper."

The boy looked interested. "You live at the zoo? For real? That's pretty sweet."

She nodded. "Yeah, it is." She looked at him expectantly. "Who are you?"

The boy recoiled, suddenly bouncing to his feet. He

tossed the flattened cup into a garbage can. "Nobody," he said.

He started down the path toward the elephant house. "Thanks for the lunch," he called over his shoulder.

"Sure," Lizzie said. "See you around."

The boy didn't answer and he didn't look back.

Chapter 4

LIKE
FATHER,
LIKE DAUGHTER

THAT NIGHT, LIZZIE heated a pot of water on the stove to make spaghetti and waited for her father to come home. The Durango house was a large bungalow on one of the maintenance roads at the edge of the zoo property. A big sign at the beginning of the long gravel drive said AUTHORIZED VEHICLES ONLY—NO TRESPASSING. On rare occasions, visitors would walk down the road by mistake, but the fact that it was gravel, rather than paved, combined with the absence of any zoo animals and the distance to the house, usually persuaded them to turn around. The house had a big porch across the front with white wicker furniture and a swing. It was painted yellow, with green shutters, because those had been Lizzie's mother's favorite colors (or so Lizzie had been told).

Lizzie's mother had died right after she was born—in the hospital, the very night after Lizzie's birth. She had something called preeclampsia, which was a kind of high blood pressure some women got when they were pregnant. It could be treated, but Lizzie's mother's wasn't diagnosed in time, and she'd had a seizure and died.

Of course, Lizzie had no memory of this, or of her mother, Clare. There were several photos from the hospital, with her mother in a pale floral-print hospital gown, cuddling a little pink-blanketed log against her chest. The pink log was Lizzie. Her mother looked pale and exhausted, her forehead shiny with sweat. But she was smiling, and Lizzie's father, leaning into the frame of the photo, beamed with joy.

Sometimes Lizzie would stare and stare at these pictures, because, after all, there she was, in her mother's arms, and that moment had to have been preserved somehow, somewhere, in her distant memory. But try as she might, she could remember nothing about her mother . . . not her smell, not her voice, not her touch.

She had come to realize that this was one of the terrible things about dead mothers: You would miss them for the rest of your life, even if you'd never known them. Sometimes Lizzie would look at pictures of her pretty mother, with her sun-streaked hair and big laughing eyes, and allow herself to imagine, just for a minute, what it would be like to wrap her arms around her. But even thinking about that gave her a shivery, dangerous feeling, like holding your hand too close to a flame.

And anyway, what was the point? It had to be said: Losing your mother the day after you were born was not like losing a mother you had known and loved. Lizzie could never really feel sad about it, because her mother was not a real person to her. She had no idea what it would be like if Clare Durango were still around. Oh, occasionally, she did feel sorry for herself, in an abstract sort of way, as a kid who didn't have a mother. Whenever there were class field trips with parent chaperones, or after back-to-school night when mothers and fathers left notes on the desks, or when the Lodisto Community Center held its annual Mother-Daughter Tea: These were times when it seemed particularly bad to have no mother.

In fact, it was so often a situation that had to be explained to strangers that Lizzie occasionally called herself

an orphan. It had a romantic sound to it, like something from a fairy tale . . . though it did cause confusion at times, when her father showed up.

"Don't I count for anything?" he'd ask in mock outrage.

"Well, okay," Lizzie amended. "Not an orphan. A motherless child."

"Oh, come on, Lizzie," Mike Durango would scoff. "Where do you get this stuff? Stop being dramatic."

Mike had no patience for self-pity, but that almost made Lizzie feel sadder for her father. You could tell from the old photos that they had been a pair— Clare and Mike, Mike and Clare. Her parents had met when they were both keepers at the San Diego Zoo, one of the biggest and best zoos in the world. Her mother worked with the hoofstock, which meant antelopes, giraffes, zebras, and anything with hooves. Her father worked with the big cats. But they shared a language of zoo animals—their care and habits and quirks— and when her mother died, Lizzie had the sense that her father had lost the one person in the world who had always understood exactly what he was talking about.

When Lizzie sifted through the old photographs of her parents together, she could see an unfamiliar expression on her father's face: a happy, wide-open grin that he never wore now. Lizzie's Grandma May had commented once that it was impossible to understand who Mike was now without knowing about Clare's death; but that it was equally impossible to understand who he'd been before, all those years ago, without peeling away Clare's death like the skin of an onion. And since that was an impossible task—taking away the death of his wife as if it had never happened—Lizzie was left to believe that the old version of her father was as lost to her as her dead mother.

Lizzie's mother had been an avid horseback rider and came from a long line of women who were adventurous in the out-of-doors. In fact, a distant cousin, Clare Marie Hodges, for whom Lizzie's mother had been named, had been the first female park ranger in the country. She had worked in Yosemite in the early 1900s. She rode her horse all over the park, checking on trails, helping people who'd gotten lost or stranded. In the little second-story apartment over the Durangos' garage, where Grandma May stayed when she visited, there were old photographs and other mementos from Clare Marie Hodges's time in Yosemite. Lizzie liked to look at them. When she found herself missing her mother (or at least the idea of her mother), it was reassuring to imagine that the same love of the wild that had been in her mother's family for generations was now coursing through her own veins.

Mike Durango, however, was not one to linger in the past, or to let Lizzie do that, either. Grandma May had also told Lizzie, "Your father doesn't have a good personality for grief." When Lizzie asked what that meant, she said only, "He believes in getting on with it."

But wasn't that what everyone had to do? Lizzie wondered. What was a good personality for grief, anyway? If you got stuck in your sadness, caught in the swirling vortex of if-onlys and might-have-beens, surely it would pull you under. You might never make it to the surface again.

Fortunately, Lizzie liked her life very well just as it was. She lived at the zoo! By the time she was barely able to walk, she had bottle-fed a baby llama, ridden on an elephant, handled a boa constrictor, and stroked the velvety nose of a giraffe. She loved animals as much as her father did, and in turn, he let her see and do things at the zoo that no other kid ever got to experience. It was a lucky, fantastic life, Lizzie knew . . . and having no mother was only a very small part of it.

She was thinking about all of these things as she

boiled water in the huge stockpot and ripped open a package of spaghetti. She was also realizing that the one person she did truly miss right now was her best friend Margaret Kincaid, who was in Australia for two months visiting relatives. They were planning to Skype or e-mail each other, but the time change was so vast (Margaret was always going to bed right as Lizzie was waking up, and vice versa) that it seemed as if Margaret might as well be on another planet. Summer was the busiest time at the zoo, so there was plenty to occupy Lizzie, but it would have been much more fun with Margaret for company. And right now, it would have been especially good to be able to tell Margaret about what had happened at the snack bar with the mysterious boy.

"Hey, Lizzie."

The back door slammed and Lizzie could hear her father in the laundry room.

"Hey, Mike," she called.

Her father was Zookeeper Mike to everyone at the zoo, so Lizzie sometimes called him Mike, too. Now that she was older, she had started calling him Dad more often. People outside the zoo seemed to find it strange that she called her father by his first name, and it was often easier to conform to their expectations than to have one more thing she had to explain.

A faint smell of tiger pee drifted into the kitchen. It had a particular acrid stench that almost burned your nostrils. Mike always had to shower before dinner.

"Give me ten minutes," he called, before thudding upstairs.

Lizzie poured a jar of spaghetti sauce into a pan and began stirring it over a low flame. There were only a few dinners she could make by herself—spaghetti, soup with cheese toast, pans of store-bought casseroles or lasagnas that she only had to heat in the oven—but she cooked a couple of nights a week. Mike cooked two or three nights, often barbecuing fish or chicken on the grill in the backyard. Then they got pizza or Chinese takeout on the other nights.

As she stirred the spaghetti sauce, Lizzie thought about the boy. He had gobbled down the rest of her lunch as if he were starving. But then he had also saved some for later, and that seemed so deliberate when he was clearly very hungry . . . as if he wasn't sure when he would eat next. Between that and stealing the little kid's hamburger at the snack bar, there was something strange about him. She wondered if she'd see him again.

Her father appeared in the kitchen, rubbing his hair with a towel. He kissed the top of her head and grabbed a bunch of silverware from the drawer. "That smells great," he said. "A lot better than I do."

"You smell okay now."

"Do I? I can still smell it."

Lizzie dropped a fistful of spaghetti into the boiling water. "One of the wolves seems sick," she said.

Her father nodded grimly. "Yeah, Athena. She's not doing well."

"Do you know what's wrong with her?"

He shook his head. "She was throwing up; now she's not eating and she's having trouble standing. It came on pretty suddenly. Karen took her to the clinic."

Karen Lockport was the zoo veterinarian . . . and also Mike's sometime girlfriend. They occasionally went out to dinner, and while she never stayed over at the house, Lizzie got the impression that she might like to. Her father had dated several women over the years, but none of them ever spent the night. He kept them separate from his life with Lizzie, a division of worlds that she appreciated. She liked Karen—who was smart and intense, with the quick confidence of a doctor— but she and her father formed their own small circle of family, and she didn't want outsiders interfering with that.

"It's not something contagious, is it?" Lizzie asked. The greatest fear of zookeepers was a contagious illness that swept through a certain species. It had happened only once at the John Muir Wildlife Park; one of the otters developed a fungal respiratory disease that eventually killed all four. It was even worse when a more exotic species of animal got sick, because veterinarians had less experience treating them.

Mike shook his head. "I hope not. Maybe a reaction to something she ate. But we decided to isolate her just in case."

Lizzie watched his face, trying to gauge how worried he was. "Do you think she'll be okay?"

He grabbed two oven mitts and dumped the pot of spaghetti over a strainer in the sink as steam billowed around him. "Yeah. Yeah, I do. She seems weak, but she's alert."

Lizzie felt a wave of relief. Her father was almost always right about these things. He'd seen so many sick animals, and he usually seemed to know when they weren't going to make it. Lizzie had asked him about it once, how he could tell when they were going to die. "It's their eyes," he'd said. "They're not focused on anything. Dying animals are so deep inside themselves, they're not looking out at the world anymore."

She got two plates from the cupboard and her father forked spaghetti onto them, while she ladled the tomato sauce. This was how they were together, she and Mike . . . a team. Her father worked long hours and Lizzie was left by herself much of the time, but they had the household routines down to a science.

Now, as the blue dusk cloaked the yard, Lizzie sat at the table with Mike in the small, bright kitchen. For a minute, she considered telling him what had happened at the snack bar earlier. But then she thought about the boy, and how quickly he'd disappeared when she asked who he was. He seemed like a secret she shouldn't share. At least not yet.

Chapter 5

THE HIDEOUT

THE NEXT MORNING, Lizzie pulled on shorts and a T-shirt, quickly ran a brush through her hair, and toasted a bagel to take with her.

Mike was standing at the kitchen counter reading the newspaper. "Where are you running off to?" he asked as she gulped a glass of orange juice.

"Nowhere. I just want to check on the wolves." She slathered cream cheese on the bagel, wrapped it in a paper towel, and tucked her notebook under one arm.

"Good idea. I'll come with you."

"But you're making coffee," Lizzie protested. "It'll take too long. Meet me over there?"

Her father wavered. "Yeah, all right."

Lizzie did want to check on the wolves. But mostly she wanted to be near the front gates when the zoo opened, in case the boy came back. She was sure she'd seen him at the zoo before. Maybe he lived nearby and visited a lot in the summer. She had a feeling he came to the zoo alone, and she wanted to find out more about him.

It was just after eight o'clock when she walked down the driveway into the zoo. The morning sun was high, but the entrance gates wouldn't open for another hour. This hour of the day and the evening hours after closing were Lizzie's favorite times. The zoo was empty and silent in the early morning. Occasionally she would see one of the custodians or one of the keepers emerging from the animal houses, but mostly she felt like an explorer on a foreign continent, thousands of miles away. Dew sparkled on the clumps of flowers bordering the walkway. She passed the pink flamingos, each standing on one leg in the lake, with their curled, black-striped bills; then the herd of gazelles in the African Savannah exhibit, who turned their tiny, masked faces toward her in sync; then the crocodiles, sliding from their sandy embankment into the murky water of the moat.

The zoo animals were grouped by continent, so

within minutes, Lizzie had passed from Africa to North America. Here were the funny otters. They ran across their pen as she drew near, their sleek backs undulating, making their strange chirping noise. She clucked her tongue at them. They paused to stare at her with beady eyes, then slipped into the water, twisting and curling around each other, already hard at play.

Lizzie passed the prairie dog exhibit. The prairie dogs were all still underground, so their habitat looked like nothing more than a dusty hummock of earth. Now she could see Wolf Woods. As usual, the wolves were at the back of the enclosure, under the stand of pines. She counted six. For a minute, she scanned the large field in concern. Then she remembered that Athena had been taken to the clinic.

Four of the wolves were standing; two were lying down. Even at a distance, Lizzie could pick out Lobo immediately. He stood apart from the others, ears pricked, watching her. Lizzie dropped into her usual position on the rock near the curb and opened her notebook across her knees. She took a bite of the still-warm bagel, licking the cream cheese off her fingers. She knew not to whistle or snap at the wolves. They weren't pets. She just wanted to watch them, not interfere with their normal behavior.

She uncapped her pen and began to write.

July 27, 8:15 a.m. Wolf Woods. The pack is gathered beneath the pine trees in the rear corner of the pen. There are only six of them now because Athena is sick and in the clinic. I hope she gets better soon! I wonder how it is for the others, not knowing where she is or what's happened to her.

Lizzie knew that certain animals mourned their dead. She wasn't sure about wolves, but her father had told her that elephants did. They would sometimes stand watch over their dead relatives, bury them with leaves and branches, show deep sadness, and even shed tears. The zoo visitors loved hearing these stories—anything that made the animals seem more like humans. Lizzie herself felt impatient with those comparisons, though. It seemed wrong somehow to assume that animals experienced the same emotions as humans, and even more wrong to believe that animal feelings only mattered if they could be understood in human terms.

She looked up and gasped. Lobo was standing in front of her, a few feet from the fence. He'd crossed the enclosure in the time it had taken her to write those few sentences, and he had done it in utter silence. It was all too easy to imagine how swiftly and silently the wolves could track and kill their prey. As Lizzie watched, his ears flattened, and the ruff of his fur stiffened. Startled, she glanced around and saw Mike walking toward her. When she turned back, Lobo had retreated to join the rest of the pack.

"He's not used to me yet," Mike said. He stood behind her, his coffee mug cupped in both hands, a wisp of steam rising. "Maybe he prefers women. He seems more comfortable with you and Karen. He's settled in better than the others, don't you think?"

Lizzie nodded. "He's the only one who comes to the fence. The rest stay in the back."

Mike sighed. "It's not a good place for them, this pen."

Lizzie looked at him, puzzled. "But it's so big compared to the others."

"Yeah, it's the best we can do. But wolves roam. In the wild, they cover twenty, thirty miles in a day, sometimes a lot more than that . . . and the territory for a pack can be several hundred square miles. So even if this pen looks big compared to some of our other ones, for a wolf, it's probably the equivalent of a closet."

Lizzie looked at him in horror. "That's awful! Why does the zoo even have wolves, then?"

"Conservation," Mike answered. "It's to protect them. You know the story with these guys . . . They were all injured or trapped up north. Some of them were caught killing cattle or sheep. If we don't keep them here, safe, they'll end up shot or poisoned."

Lizzie lapsed into silence, thinking that this was another reason her father was called a "keeper." It didn't just mean to hold on to something, to keep an animal in a cage. It meant to keep safe, to keep alive, to tend to and care for. But in this case, keeping the wolves meant sacrificing something else.

Her father took a last swallow of coffee. "This pen isn't perfect," he said. "But it's better than the alternative."

Lizzie sighed, not at all sure. At least if the wolves were in the wild, they were free to run and hunt and roam as far as they wanted. They might not live as long—they might not live long at all—but wasn't the life itself better than the one they would lead in a cage at the zoo?

"Hey." Mike tugged her ponytail. "Don't worry. They'll get used to this place soon enough. Karen wants to rehabilitate these guys in the wild at some point, so who knows, maybe that will happen one day."

"Really?" Lizzie squinted up at him, suddenly hopeful. "Could she do that?"

"Well, not anytime soon. Not after what we paid for the new exhibit. The board of directors won't allow it. But she's pretty determined, so maybe in a few years."

"Oh." Lizzie frowned, closing her notebook. A few years sounded like a long time to spend in a place that felt like a closet.

"Okay, I have work to do. See you tonight."

"Bye," Lizzie called as her father strode down the path toward the Rain Forest exhibit.

The sun was bright and it was nearly nine o'clock. Lizzie decided to position herself close to the zoo entrance and watch for the boy. She carried her notebook and the remaining half of her bagel, now cold, and settled herself on one of the benches. Two teenagers were working the cash registers at the gate, and a bunch of families were already lined up outside. So it began, another summer day at the zoo. Within an hour, Lizzie knew, the place would be filled with people, families with young children, couples strolling together, the occasional elderly person who almost always came alone, walking quietly from exhibit to exhibit, lost in thought.

She hoped the boy would come. Biting into the bagel, she watched as the crowds streamed through the gates.

After an hour, Lizzie was bored and uncomfortable. The wooden slats of the bench were biting into the backs of her thighs, the sun was hot, and her hands were sticky with cream cheese. Even though she'd been trying to write down little observations of the people— with the thought that humans were a part of nature, too—she hadn't seen anything all that interesting, much less remarkable. She stood and stretched, wadding up the paper towel and tossing it in the trash can, ready to give up.

But then something caught her eye.

It was a blue shirt.

It wasn't coming through the entrance gates. It was behind her, flitting around the corner of the elephant house. Lizzie turned and shielded her eyes with one hand. She'd only seen a glimpse of it, and now the blue shirt was darting between groups of people until it disappeared altogether. She started walking quickly, not certain that she'd seen it at all.

When she got to the elephant house, she looked around. A ragged line of people clustered against the high concrete wall, hoisting toddlers high in the air, calling to Timbo and Belle. The elephants stood in their dusty yard, each one's head aligned to the other's rump, patiently swishing flies away with their stringy tails.

It had been the boy, hadn't it? It had looked like the same blue shirt . . . which was odd, wasn't it? Why would he be wearing the same shirt? And he hadn't been standing on the path, in front of the wall where you could see the elephants. He'd come from *behind* the elephant house, from a wooded area where the public wasn't allowed. There wasn't anything there, as far as Lizzie knew. It didn't make sense.

She surveyed the crowd one more time. No blue shirt. *Okay, then,* she thought. *Let's see what's behind the elephant house.* She waited until nobody was looking in her direction, then quickly hopped over the wooden guard-rail and ran through the brush, around the corner of the big concrete building.

It was dark and shaded behind the building. At first all she saw was the thick shrubbery, punctuated by an occasional small tree, struggling toward the sunlight. She began to poke around, peering into the foliage.

Then she gasped.

Against the wall of the elephant house, tucked under the dense bushes, was an old, dirty blanket. As Lizzie approached it, she saw something else: a soda can. Then an empty, grease-stained paper plate creased with folds— her pizza plate from yesterday! When she bent down and looked more closely, she could see a backpack, shoved deep into the mass of twiggy branches.

TYLER

LIZZIE SURVEYED THE scene. The boy was clearly sleeping here, or at least staying here. The blanket, the backpack, the can of soda—how long had he been taking refuge in this hideout? She tried to think what to do next. She could track him down, or wait here and surprise him. But it was only mid-morning now, and there seemed few things more boring than sitting in the dark shrubbery behind the elephant house. She decided to scout around and see if she could find him.

The zoo walkways were now full of people. Lizzie listened to snippets of conversation: "Oh, look at his BIG trunk! How'd you like that to wrap around you and squeeze you tight?" "Mommy! Pick me up! I want to SEE!" "What does a monkey say? Oooo-oooo, aaah-aaah."

Zoo visitors always took great delight in imitating the animals—either their movements or the noises they made. It was true that Lizzie herself did this with the otters and an old macaw parrot in the Rain Forest, but she prided herself on really sounding like the animals, to the point where the macaw would squawk back at her. Other people seemed to just be clowning around. Anyone could tell that the black-and-white colobus monkeys didn't say "oooo-oooo, aaah-aaah" any more than a pig said "oink."

Lizzie wandered down the path, into the sea of colorful summer shirts. Where was the boy? Then she had an idea. If he'd just gotten up, maybe he was at the snack bar, scrounging for food again. She wended her way through a gridlock of strollers and ran down the hill to the food court.

She saw him immediately. He was sitting at one of the tables, eating a carton of french fries. He had his back to her, so he didn't have a chance to escape before she slipped into the chair next to him.

The boy jumped in surprise. He curled his arm protectively around the french fries. "What are you doing here?"

"I live here, remember?" Lizzie gestured at the fries. "Did you find those on a table?"

"No," the boy mumbled. "I bought these." He shoved a handful of fries into his mouth, chewing noisily.

Lizzie studied him. "If you had money, why didn't you buy yourself lunch yesterday?"

He glared at her. "Didn't have enough."

A sudden pit of sympathy opened up in Lizzie's stomach. She looked at him, and her expression seemed to irritate him.

"What do you want?" he demanded.

"Nothing," she said.

"Then why are you following me?"

Lizzie felt her cheeks grow hot.

"I'm not." She watched him eat the last french fry.

"Quit staring at me," he grunted, getting up and rubbing his palms on his shorts.

Lizzie stood, too. "Are you still hungry?" she asked. "I can get free food . . . you know, because my dad works here."

The boy's dark eyes bored into her. "For real?"

She nodded.

"And you don't have to pay?"

"Nope."

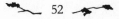

"Sweet," he said softly.

"Do you want something?" Lizzie asked.

The boy shot a quick glance at the large menu over the snack bar, then back at Lizzie. "Well, I'm pretty full up," he said nonchalantly. "But, you know, if it's free, I could probably eat a hamburger."

"Sure." Lizzie started to walk to the counter to order.

"With onion rings. And maybe a vanilla milk shake. I love milk shakes." He grinned, and she could see his face open up finally, shining with anticipation.

"Okay, a hamburger and a milk shake." Lizzie walked up to the cash register. It was too early for the lunch crush, so there was no line.

Sonya, one of the women who worked there, smiled at her. "You're here early, Lizzie. What can I get you?"

"A hamburger with onion rings and a vanilla milk shake, please," Lizzie told her.

"And one of those giant cookies, too," the boy called.

"What kind?"

"You choose," he answered magnanimously. "Something with chocolate."

"Who's your friend?" Sonya asked. "He's here a lot."

"Just some boy," Lizzie answered awkwardly.

"From school?" Sonya continued, loading a plastic tray and pushing it across the counter toward Lizzie. "He must live in town."

Lizzie nodded vaguely. "Thanks, Sonya. See you later."

She walked back to the table and had barely set down the tray before the boy was ripping the foil off the hamburger and cramming it into his mouth. "Mmmm," he mumbled, mouth full. "Nice and hot." He hesitated, then thrust it toward her. "Want some?"

Lizzie shook her head, watching with a mixture of wonder and fascination as he devoured it. Once again, he stopped short of finishing it, which seemed to take a conscious effort, and wrapped the remainder in a piece of foil.

He took a long slurp of the milk shake and leaned back in his chair. "So you can do this any old day at all? Just come down here and get food for free?"

Lizzie nodded.

He said something under his breath and shook his head. "That is some life. I mean, you are *lucky*, you know?"

"Yeah, it's pretty great," Lizzie agreed.

"Onion ring?" He tilted the cardboard carton toward her.

She didn't really feel like eating an onion ring so soon after her breakfast, but it seemed like maybe this was a test of something. She remembered what her father had told her about food sharing among animals . . . that it was an expression of friendship or a sign of allegiance.

"Sure," she said, taking a small one. "So . . ." She hesitated. "I know where you're staying. Behind the elephant house."

The boy stiffened and stared at her. "What are you talking about? I am not. I just . . . I come here first thing, most mornings. I like walking around. By myself," he added. He scanned the plaza anxiously.

"I didn't tell anyone," Lizzie said, "if that's what you're worried about."

His eyebrows furrowed. "I'm not worried." He quickly sucked down the rest of his milk shake. Then he balled up his trash, tossing it in a nearby bin, and stood up. Gathering what was left of his hamburger, along with the cookie, he said, "See you around."

"I haven't told anyone *yet*," Lizzie said, watching him.

"What's your problem?" he snapped, leaning over her. "Why don't you just leave me alone? You come here

anytime you want, get your food all day for free. What do you know about anything?"

Lizzie stood up, too, looking straight into his wary face. "Stop yelling. Just tell me who you are. Maybe I can help you."

"Help me? Help *me*? I don't need your help."

He stomped angrily across the plaza.

She ran right after him.

"Come on. I can get you food. I can find you a better place to stay. I grew up here! Just tell me who you are."

He was walking quickly now, almost running, but he slowed down and looked at her. "Why? Why would you do that? You don't even know me."

She shrugged. The truth was, she couldn't say why she wanted so badly to help him. But the thought of him sleeping on the cold ground, in the bushes behind the elephant house, made her feel desperate to do something.

He kept staring at her, his brows knitted over his big eyes. She liked his face, even when he was scowling at her . . . the smooth, warm brown of it framed by wiry curls.

He turned and started walking again, but more slowly.

Lizzie kept pace with him. "What's your name?"

There was a long silence. "Tyler," he said finally. "Tyler Briggs."

"I'm Lizzie Durango."

"You told me that already."

"Where's your family?" She knew better than to ask where he lived, because clearly the zoo was where he lived now. But how long had he been here? He was skinny, but a natural kind of skinny. He didn't look like he was starving.

He glared at her. "I don't have one," he said.

"Sure you do," Lizzie coaxed. "Everyone has a family. Even if you're mad at them."

"Well, I don't."

"I don't have a mom," Lizzie offered. "But I have a dad, and I live with him. So who do you live with? I mean, before you . . . came here."

"Foster family," he muttered. "And I'm not going back there."

Lizzie studied his profile. "Oh."

They kept walking, and Lizzie saw that they were headed in the direction of the elephant house. Was he taking her back to his hideout?

"Did something happen to your mom and dad?" she asked.

His face clouded with anger. "Everything that happened to them, they did to themselves."

Lizzie looked at him blankly. "What do you mean?"

But Tyler only stared at the ground and marched ahead of her.

She tried a different tack. "Well . . . what's wrong with your foster family? Why did you run away?"

"I didn't run away!" he snapped. "I just, you know, came down here for a while. For a break."

"Okay, okay," Lizzie said. "Don't get mad. Were they mean to you or something?"

He shook his head. "Nah. They're fine. But they got six other kids living in that house. Well, five since Jesse left. And anyway, they go to church all the time. I'm done with that."

"Who's Jesse?" Lizzie asked. It seemed like the first personal thing he'd said, a clue dangling in front of her. If she followed it, she thought it might lead back to something important.

But Tyler's mouth clapped shut.

"Six kids," Lizzie said, trying to keep him talking. "That's a lot."

"Yeah. They won't even know I'm gone." He walked faster.

As they came up the rise toward the elephant house,

Belle turned toward them and flapped her ears. Lizzie had seen her do this when her keeper approached, a happy greeting. The huge elephant ambled across the dusty yard, looking straight at Tyler.

Lizzie stared at him, and she could see his face change. He started to smile in spite of himself. "The elephants know you," she said in disbelief.

"Well, duh," Tyler said. "This is where I hang out."

Belle came to the edge of the moat and stretched her long, sinuous trunk toward the railing, while the crowd of tourists shrieked in delight.

Lizzie looked from the elephant back to Tyler, suddenly indignant. "You've been feeding her! That's why she's excited to see you."

He shrugged. "Not much. I throw her a french fry sometimes."

"You can't do that. It'll make her sick."

"I'm careful," he said. "I don't give her meat or anything."

Lizzie shuddered, thinking of what her father would say. Tyler picked up a stick from the ground and walked over to the railing. He stepped onto its lowest rung and leaned far into space, stretching out his arm, waving the stick. On the other side of the moat, Belle's trunk felt through the air, for all the world like a hand reaching

 59

toward him. The rubbery tip curled around the branch and tugged gently, pulling it from Tyler's grip.

The crowd whooped, and Lizzie could see Tyler's shy grin of delight. She briefly worried that Belle would pull him forward over the wall—the elephants, as gentle as they were, had amazing strength—but when Belle realized he wasn't holding any food, she turned away,

sweeping the branch back and forth over the dusty ground.

"Hey, kid, you're not supposed to do that," a man said sharply, and Tyler stepped down from the railing.

"Sorry," he mumbled, in the voice of someone used to being scolded.

He waited until the throng of people turned their attention back to the elephants, then motioned to Lizzie.

"C'mon," he said softly, walking along the fence toward the side of the elephant enclosure.

Together, they slipped over the railing and ran through the bushes to the wooded area behind the elephant house.

A SAFE PLACE

WADING INTO THE shrubbery, Tyler began gathering his things. He shook the blanket and a shower of dust, grass, and tiny twigs rained down. It didn't look nearly comfortable enough to sleep on, Lizzie thought.

"What are you doing?" she asked.

"Moving my stuff," he said, as if it were obvious. "I can't stay here now that you found it."

"But I told you I wouldn't say anything."

"Why should I believe you? And anyway, if you figured out I'm here, it's only a matter of time before somebody else does." He glanced at her resentfully, tucking the leftover hamburger and the cookie into the backpack.

Lizzie knelt on the hard ground and scooped up the trash. "How long have you been—" She started to say "living here," but he seemed so sensitive about the implications of that, she changed it to "staying here?"

"Not long."

"A week? A month?"

"No!" Tyler snorted, as if the very idea were absurd. He rolled up the blanket and tucked it under one arm, hoisting the strap of the backpack over his shoulder.

Lizzie didn't want him to leave. Most of all, she didn't want to be the reason he left. She tried to keep him talking.

"Why'd you come here? I mean, the zoo."

He looked at her in surprise. "It feels safe. No cops around. No people who'd be watching me."

Lizzie nodded. That seemed true. The zoo was like the beach or the playground or the movie theater. Everybody was there for a happy reason.

"And . . ." Tyler hesitated, as if deciding how much to tell her. "I came here last summer for camp. Jesse was one of the counselors, and they let me come, cuz I like animals. I like animals better than people."

Lizzie smiled at him. "Me too," she said. She knew about the zoo day camp; it was popular with the local schoolkids, who got to run around the zoo playing games and learning about the animals. Maybe that's why Tyler looked familiar to her. It occurred to her suddenly that maybe one reason he felt comfortable at the zoo was that the animals were kind of like him—out of place, away from where they really wanted to be.

"Is Jesse your brother?" she asked.

Tyler's face closed. "No. I told you, I don't got a family."

"But then where will you go?" she persisted.

He shrugged. "Maybe somewhere in town."

"That doesn't sound good," Lizzie said, worried. "You can't just be a homeless person."

"I'm not homeless!" Tyler snapped. "I'm . . . between places."

"Okay, okay." She took the blanket from him, ignoring his resistance. "Listen. Come with me. I know where we can go." And in a moment of inspiration, she did. The garage apartment! It was never used except when her grandmother visited. Her father wouldn't even know Tyler was there.

"We? There's no 'we,' " Tyler answered.

"Okay, *you*," Lizzie said. "Don't you want free food

and a place to stay? I have a great idea." She could see his resolve faltering. "Oh, just come on, Tyler."

"Where are we going?"

"Back to my house," Lizzie told him. "My dad and I live right here at the zoo, and we have an apartment over the garage that we only use when my grandma comes to visit. You can stay up there."

"What? That's worse than here! Somebody will see me."

"No, it's down a long driveway."

Tyler looked unconvinced. "But what about your dad? Nobody can know I'm there. For real."

"Yeah, I get it."

"If anybody finds out, they'll send me back."

Lizzie sighed. "Listen, my dad never goes up there. He won't know as long as you don't make a lot of noise or have the light on at night. And after he leaves for work, you can do whatever you want."

When Tyler still hesitated, Lizzie groaned in frustration. "Don't you want to? It'll be so much better than this, I promise."

He settled his backpack on his shoulder and looked around. "Nobody bothered me here. Until you. And I made friends with the elephants."

"Well, they'll still be your friends. You know what they say about elephants—"

"Yeah, I know what they say," he interrupted. "Elephants never forget."

He stood, not moving, and for a minute, Lizzie thought he was going to refuse. But then he said, "Okay. Let's go."

So they hurried around the corner of the building. A man pushing a double stroller glanced at them curiously as they stepped over the guardrail. Lizzie dumped her armload of trash into one of the bins.

"This way," she said, leading Tyler down the path in the direction of her house.

As they passed the sprawling brick building that housed the tropical rain forest, Tyler said, "Hey, let's cut through here."

"Sure," Lizzie agreed. They pushed through the double doors into the warm fog of air. They were immediately surrounded by lush jungle. A wide boardwalk wound its way through leafy trees and huge, tropical flowers, while high above, colorful birds swooped and chattered. The walkway was crowded with people, but Tyler maneuvered confidently to the area by the exit. Here, behind a glass window, the big turquoise-and-gold macaw clutched the limb of a tree. It stared at them.

Tyler's face broke into a grin and he bobbed his head

up and down. The parrot immediately bobbed its head in response.

Lizzie looked at him in surprise.

"Yeah, I taught it how to do that," he said casually.

"You did?" She'd been hoping she could get the parrot to squawk at them, but that no longer seemed so impressive.

"And I'll show you something else," Tyler said. His voice sounded eager in a way Lizzie hadn't heard before.

He crossed the exhibit area to the viewing window for the pygmy marmosets. Of all the rain forest animals, these tiny monkeys were Lizzie's favorites, small enough to fit inside a person's hand. They were shy and often darted into the holes of their tree-trunk home, but it was fun to watch them scamper and hide.

When Lizzie and Tyler approached the glass, the two monkeys were huddled inside their burrow, their tiny, intense faces peeking out of the darkness.

"Shhhh, watch," Tyler whispered. "I'll get them to come out."

He stood very still and made a soft clicking noise with his tongue. The monkeys cocked their heads and blinked their bright eyes. After a few seconds, one poked its head out of the hole, watching Tyler.

Slowly, Tyler walked to the other side of the window, still clicking his tongue. Suddenly, both monkeys emerged, running along the tree branch, following him.

"See? These little guys love me," he said happily.

Just then, a bunch of kids rushed over, elbowing Lizzie aside.

"Look!"

"The monkeys are out now!"

"Mommy, come see."

With the commotion, the monkeys promptly dove for cover, and Lizzie and Tyler also fled, through the exit doors into the dry summer heat.

"You must go there all the time," Lizzie said in amazement. "I mean, I do, too, but—" She didn't want to admit that she'd never figured out how to lure the marmosets into leaving their burrow.

"Well, I can't get in at night," Tyler said. "They lock the doors. But yeah, I like the Rain Forest. It feels like someplace really far away, you know?"

Lizzie nodded, and in that instant she understood why, for Tyler, the zoo had seemed such a good place to run away to. It was so different from anywhere else, a total escape.

"This is a shortcut," she told Tyler, stepping over

a guardrail and leading the way through the bushes behind the Barnyard.

As usual, the goats trotted over to the fence, full of curiosity. Tyler stopped to scratch their heads, and they butted under his hand.

"Okay," Lizzie said, feeling a little annoyed. "Are there any animals here you *haven't* made friends with?"

He grinned at her helplessly. "Hey, I'm king of the zoo."

"The goats are interested in everybody," Lizzie said dismissively. "See? They like me too." She stroked their wiry fur.

"Well, that's probably just cuz you live here," Tyler said. "They're used to you. They actually like me." He was still smiling, and she couldn't tell if he was teasing her.

"What about the wolves?" she said. She thought of Lobo and the way he came up to the fence and watched her. Did he do that with Tyler, too?

Tyler shook his head. "Nah, they stay way in the back," he said, and she felt a rush of relief. "Plus, there are always people in that cage," he added.

Lizzie turned to him, startled. "What do you mean?"

He shrugged. "Just what I said. Even at night I've seen people in there. So I don't hang out by the wolves cuz I don't want anyone to see me."

Lizzie frowned. "I don't know who'd be in Wolf

Woods at night. Maybe you saw one of the custodians cleaning up? But they're never inside the pen."

Tyler seemed unperturbed. "All I'm saying is, I see a lot of stuff around here after dark that nobody else sees." He started to say more, but then seemed to change his mind.

"Well, I *live* here." Lizzie glared at him. "So I'm sure you haven't seen more stuff than I have." Who did he think he was? Bragging about being king of the zoo.

"If you say so," Tyler answered, clearly unconvinced. "Where's your house, anyway?"

"We would have been there already if you didn't keep stopping," Lizzie told him. She strode through the bushes in the direction of home.

As they walked down the long drive, Tyler looked around with interest. "So you live back here? Inside the zoo?"

"Yep," Lizzie said.

"For your whole life?"

"Well, not when I was a baby. But for as long as I can remember, I've lived here with my dad."

"What happened to your mom?"

"She died right after I was born."

"How'd she die?"

His voice was so matter-of-fact, Lizzie glanced at him. She didn't mind talking about it, but most people treated her mother's death with a respectful, sympathetic hush. "She had a seizure."

"What's that?"

Lizzie considered how to describe it. "I think it's when something happens inside your brain, and your heart stops or you can't breathe."

"Why'd that happen to her?"

"She had some problem, being pregnant with me, and the doctors didn't know it until she had me and then she had the seizure."

Tyler thought for a minute. "So she died because of you?"

Lizzie stared at him. But his expression was only curious, as if he genuinely wanted to know.

"No," she said firmly. "She died because of being pregnant and having some disease."

"Being pregnant with you," Tyler persisted.

"Well, yeah," Lizzie said. "But it's not like I killed her. I was a baby. She just died."

He seemed to be thinking about that. "Okay," he said finally. "Hey! Is that the place I'm going to stay?" The little yellow house had come into view, and some distance behind it, the garage, with its second floor full of windows.

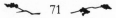

"Yeah, that's it," Lizzie said.

Tyler gave a low whistle. "Sweet!" he said. "That will be way better than sleeping on the ground."

"Told you," Lizzie said happily. As they walked past the quiet house, Tyler asked in a low voice, "Are you sure your dad's not here?"

"No, he's at work." Lizzie ran straight to the side door of the garage and picked up one of the flowerpots near the stoop. "Here's the key."

She dangled the brass key in front of him before inserting it into the lock and turning. She had to push her shoulder against the door, which had warped a little over the years. It stuck against the doorjamb. Whenever Grandma May visited, she deliberately didn't close it all the way, so that she could get in and out more easily.

"It's kind of hard to close," Lizzie said. "But you'll have to really shut it or my dad will know someone's been inside."

"No problem, I can handle that," Tyler said.

When they stepped into the dark stairwell, he slammed the door behind them.

"Wait," Lizzie protested. "Now I can't see." She felt along the wall for the light switch, but Tyler pushed past her and ran up the stairs. He opened the door at the top and sunlight spilled into the stairwell.

"Whoa! Swee-eee-eeeet!" he crowed. "This is AMAZING!"

Lizzie trotted up the stairs behind him, through swirling motes of dust caught in the sunlight. She stepped into the living room of the apartment and glanced with satisfaction at the bright, neat square of the room. "Well, it's really small, but—"

"Are you kidding me?" Tyler had raced to the opposite side and was kneeling on the faded blue sofa, looking out the windows into the yard. "This is the nicest place I've ever seen! It has a kitchen and everything!"

The apartment smelled vaguely of mildew. It had been shut up all through the rainy spring and early summer, and the dampness seemed to seep into the walls and take hold there. But it was a cheerful little place. There were big windows on three sides, looking out at the woods, the driveway, and the main house, and they were bordered by pretty flowered curtains that Grandma May had sewn herself. In addition to the blue sofa, there was a puffy, oversized armchair; a coffee table; a multicolored oval rag rug; and two big bookshelves filled with books, framed pictures, and photo albums. Abutting the living room, along the rear wall, was a little kitchen with a sink, stovetop, and microwave;

and pushed up against the window facing Lizzie's house were a table and two chairs.

Lizzie gestured down a short hall to a room that was barely big enough for a double bed. "That's the bedroom," she said. Then she opened a door off the hallway. "And here's the bathroom and the washer and dryer. We can wash your stuff if you want."

"Yes! That would be great," Tyler said. He spun around and pumped his fist in the air. "I can't believe this. I can stay here, for real? And we can keep it a secret from your dad?"

Lizzie felt a pang of guilt. She didn't keep secrets from her dad. There was hardly ever any reason to. But in this case, she knew she wouldn't have to lie to him. He would never think to ask her anything about the apartment.

"Definitely," she told Tyler. "You'll be safe here."

The afternoon was spent getting Tyler settled. Lizzie thought it was not so different from getting Grandma May settled when she came for a long visit—except that Tyler brought nothing with him besides a blanket and a dirty old backpack.

Lizzie went from room to room opening the

windows. The soft summer air rushed in, with the faint, sweet scent of jasmine. She turned on the washing machine. As warm water flooded the tub, she poured in a generous cup of detergent.

"Just throw all your stuff in here," she said. Lizzie had done the laundry for Mike and herself for years. Usually she would separate the dark and light clothes, but Tyler's stuff was mostly dark—if not in original color, then from dirt—and there was too little of it to justify another load. She pushed the grimy blanket into the fluff of white suds.

Tyler handed her a couple of sodden T-shirts, some underwear, and a pair of shorts that had been shoved deep down in the backpack.

"What about the clothes you're wearing?" Lizzie asked. "Your socks are really dirty."

"Yeah, I forgot socks," Tyler said. "When I left," he added. He looked doubtful. "Then I won't have anything to wear."

"I can give you a T-shirt and gym shorts," Lizzie said.

Tyler grimaced. "I'm not wearing girl clothes."

Lizzie rolled her eyes. "They're not girl clothes. They're zoo shirts and shorts from the gift shop. They're for anybody."

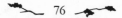 76

His eyes narrowed. "Okay, but if they look girly, forget it."

"You're in no position to be fussy," she told him. It was something her grandmother would say, and she felt like she was summoning Grandma May's spirit, here in the bright little apartment, as she cleaned and put everything in order.

"All right," Tyler said, sounding more solicitous. "I'll take a shower and you can wash these, too." He went into the bathroom and closed the door. A minute later, he opened it a few inches and dropped an armful of dirty clothes on the floor. "Thanks!" he yelled over the roar of the water.

"Is there shampoo and soap in there?" Lizzie asked.

"Yeah, it's got *everything*," he answered jubilantly.

Lizzie dropped the rest of the clothing into the washing machine. There was something deeply satisfying about watching the water darken and the suds turn gray as the clothes sloshed back and forth.

"Can I wash your backpack, too?" she called to him. The backpack was filthy, but she wasn't sure it was the kind of thing you could wash.

"Yeah, I guess," Tyler answered. "But take everything out of it."

Lizzie unzipped all the pockets and shook the

backpack over the floor. Out fell a handful of coins, two crumpled dollar bills, a pen, and two sticks of chewing gum. She reached inside the outer pocket and felt around to see if there was anything else. Her fingers grazed a piece of paper, tattered at the edges. Gently, she drew it out. It was a photograph.

Chapter 8

PICTURING THE PAST

GINGERLY, LIZZIE CARRIED the photograph into the living room and set it down on the coffee table. It was a picture of a teenage girl with long, straight blond hair, laughing down at a skinny brown baby in her lap. The baby had dark shining eyes, and he was looking straight at the camera. Tyler. She recognized him instantly. But who was the girl? A babysitter? Someone from his foster family? The photograph was creased, with frayed edges; it looked like it had been handled a thousand times. Something told Lizzie that Tyler would not be happy she'd found it. She considered putting it back, but then she couldn't wash the backpack . . . and it was so dirty.

She shrugged to herself and picked the backpack off the hallway floor. She tossed it into the washing machine and slammed the metal lid.

"I'll get you some clothes from the house," she called to Tyler.

"Okay," he yelled back. "I'm going to stay in here a while longer." She could hear him humming happily in the bathroom. She wondered how long it had been since he showered.

In her house, Lizzie quickly found a large white T-shirt with the colorful zoo logo on the front—a silhouette of John Muir surrounded by a bear, a wolf, and a parrot. She snatched it from her drawer along with a pair of navy gym shorts, and then raided Mike's top drawer for socks. As she climbed the garage stairs to the apartment, she could hear the rush of the shower. Tyler was still humming when she set the clothes on the floor of the hallway.

"Here you go," Lizzie said. "I'm leaving them right outside the door."

"Okay," he called.

She returned to the living room to wait. Finally, she heard him turn off the shower and open the door, rustling through the pile of fresh clothes.

A minute later, he appeared, damp and glowing,

with the white T-shirt sparkling against his skin. "It's kind of big," he said. "But it's okay for now."

Then he saw the photograph.

He frowned and snatched it from the table. "Hey! What were you doing going through my stuff?"

"It was in your backpack," Lizzie said. "It fell out."

Tyler glared at her. Folding the photo in half, he shoved it in the pocket of the shorts.

"Who is that?" Lizzie asked.

He didn't say anything.

"She's pretty."

Tyler took a breath, his expression wary. "It's my mom."

Lizzie couldn't hide her surprise. "It is?"

"Yeah. I know, she doesn't look like me. My dad is black." He sounded tired suddenly, as if it was something he'd had to explain many times before.

"No," Lizzie said quickly, flooded with embarrassment. "I just meant, she looks so young."

Tyler turned away. "She was eighteen when she had me."

"Well, that is young," Lizzie said. "That's only six years older than me."

He turned back to her. "Me too," he said, half smiling.

Just then the washing machine rattled loudly and

banged to a stop. Lizzie jumped up. "I'll put the clothes in the dryer."

When she came back, Tyler was standing in front of the bookcase, looking at the pictures that crowded the shelves. "There's no TV," he announced.

"No. There isn't really room for one."

"That's okay. Every house I ever been in, the TV was on all the time. It's nice to have it quiet."

He picked up a picture from the shelf in front of him and rubbed the dust off the front with his T-shirt. "Who's this?" he asked.

Lizzie took the framed photograph. "That's Grandma May. My mother's mother, the one who stays here." She looked at Grandma May's delicately lined face, the crinkles that fanned her blue eyes. Lizzie knew that hardly anybody liked the signs of age, that wrinkles were supposed to be a bad thing, and some people would do almost anything to cover them up . . . but she loved the way her grandmother's face looked. She liked the pattern of thin lines, so much more interesting than smooth skin, with their little forks and valleys, their history. And she liked the thin, crinkled, bluish skin of Grandma May's eyelids. It was so delicate. It made her feel protective toward her grandmother.

Tyler had moved on to another photo. "What about this one? It looks really old."

Lizzie took it and tilted it toward the sunlight. It was a faded black-and-white picture of a serious-looking young woman in a skirt, blouse, and hat, sitting astride a horse in a wide, grassy meadow.

"That's a cousin of my grandmother's, Clare Marie Hodges," she told him. "My mom was named for her. She was the first woman park ranger ever. She worked in Yosemite. My grandma worshipped her."

"Really?" Tyler took the photo back and stared at it. "Cool. How come there weren't women park rangers?"

"It was, like, a hundred years ago," Lizzie said. "They didn't let women do that kind of thing back then. Until her."

"So she rode a horse in Yosemite?"

"Yeah. And did park ranger stuff, like checking on the trails."

Tyler set the photograph back on the bookshelf. "How about this one?" he asked, taking down another black-and-white photo, this time of a tall, rickety wooden shack surrounded by trees.

"I don't know," Lizzie said. "Just some old cabin, I guess."

"It kind of looks like a tree house," Tyler said, squinting at the picture. "See how many levels it has?"

Lizzie looked more closely. It did appear to have two or three floors, and jutting out of the top was a little shed that looked like a human-size birdhouse.

"It's cool," Tyler decided. "We could make something like that. If we had the wood."

Lizzie stared at him, startled both by the suggestion and the way he was now including her in his plans. She loved the idea of a tree house. She imagined sitting high in the branches, with the zoo unfolding before her like a colorful map. She could take her notebook up there and write and write about everything she saw. But even while lost in this reverie, she realized there was no possible way for them to build a tree house in the yard as long as Tyler had to be kept hidden.

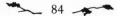

Tyler must have realized the same thing, because he abruptly set the picture back on the bookshelf. "So where am I going to sleep?" he asked, wandering down the hall to the bedroom.

Lizzie followed him. This was the room that made her miss her grandmother the most. It was so small and tidy, with its white eyelet curtains, crisp coverlet, and four pillows lined up at the top of the bed. There wasn't even space for a nightstand, but a little lamp was attached to one wall, so you could read in bed. Tyler sat on the edge of the thick mattress and bounced a couple of times.

"It's a lot better than the elephant house, right?" Lizzie asked.

"Yeah!" He flopped backward and grinned at the ceiling. "This is the best."

"Didn't you get cold there, lying on the ground all night? And bored?"

He thought for a minute. "Cold, yeah. But not bored. I told you, there's a lot happening in the zoo at night."

Lizzie shook her head. "Tell me what you mean. You said the thing about Wolf Woods, but what else?"

Tyler rolled over on his side, tucking a pillow under his head and closing his eyes. "Well, last night, for instance," he murmured sleepily, "I was walking around,

you know, in the dark, looking at the animals. Lots of them are way more interesting at night. And then over by that gray building—" His eyes popped open. "You know the one I mean?"

"Sure," Lizzie said. "That's the vet clinic." It was a low concrete building behind a chain-link fence in the far corner of the zoo, where Karen Lockport worked.

Tyler closed his eyes again and nuzzled into the pillow. "Well, I heard a weird noise. It was so late, nobody was around, but when I looked through the fence, I saw this truck, with the engine running. And it had a cage in the back."

"That doesn't sound very strange," Lizzie said. "Except that it was at night."

Tyler sat up abruptly, tossing the pillow back to the head of the bed. "Yeah, but there was something in the cage—some animal. And someone got in the truck. And then the gate opened and whoever it was, they drove out of the zoo."

Lizzie stared at him. "With the animal in the back of the truck?"

Tyler nodded. "That's weird, right?"

"What kind of animal was it?"

He shrugged. "It was too dark. I couldn't see."

"Well, how big was the cage?"

Tyler motioned with his hands, making a sweeping rectangle in the air with a height about four feet off the ground. "Big," he said. "And long."

Lizzie shook her head, puzzled. "That doesn't make sense. Who was driving?"

"I couldn't tell."

"I can ask my dad about it."

"No, you can't," Tyler said. "You can't tell him what *I* saw."

"I know that," she said, aggrieved. "I won't say anything about you. But maybe I can ask him without getting specific."

Tyler swung his feet to the floor and bounced up. "Anyway, all I'm saying is, there's a lot that happens at the zoo after everyone leaves that you probably don't know about. Even though you live here. So that was one good thing about staying overnight behind the elephant house."

"Well, you don't really know what you saw," Lizzie countered. "But it is strange. I'll try to find out what happened."

Chapter 9

BAD NEWS

LIZZIE AND TYLER spent the day stocking the apartment with provisions. This had to be done with a certain degree of subtlety and care, so that Mike wouldn't notice anything missing from the kitchen. Basically, they could only take an item to the apartment if they were able to leave one or two duplicates remaining in the refrigerator or on the cupboard shelves. Lizzie found an old cardboard box in the basement and set it on the counter. She filled it with a half gallon of milk (leaving one in the refrigerator), a bottle of cranberry juice, a box of crackers, three snack-size bags of potato chips, two apples, a plastic jar of peanut butter, and a banana.

"There," she said, pleased at the bounty. "This should last you for a while."

"Looking good," Tyler agreed. "But what about dinner?"

He was demanding, Lizzie thought, for someone who had spent who knows how many nights sleeping outside.

"I can bring you dinner after my dad and I eat."

"Will it still be hot?"

Lizzie rolled her eyes at him.

"Just asking," he said. "It would be nice if it was hot."

They each took one side of the box and bumped awkwardly through the porch door, down the steps, and across the yard to the apartment. "You sure your dad won't come home early?" Tyler asked.

Lizzie shook her head. "He's way too busy."

"What about other people?"

"Nobody else comes all the way back here," Lizzie said. "It's our yard." They climbed the stairs to the little kitchenette and began unpacking the food and putting it away. Eventually, the dryer buzzed.

"Hey, your clothes are all finished," Lizzie said, pulling Tyler's freshly laundered backpack, blanket, and clothing out of the hot dryer and dumping them on the bed.

Tyler picked up the blue T-shirt and buried his face in it. "This smells great!" he said. "And look! My backpack is a totally different color now."

Lizzie thought the color of the backpack looked a little strange, like maybe it shouldn't have been washed with the other stuff. It had turned a streaked, murky brown. But thankfully, Tyler seemed pleased with it. "It's tie-dyed," he said.

After they'd put the food away in the kitchen, Lizzie surveyed the apartment. "Can you think of anything else?"

Tyler looked around. "Nope. This place is nice." He grinned at her. "I never had my own room before."

"It's not yours," Lizzie corrected. "It's Grandma May's. But I know she wouldn't mind . . . and anyway, it's a whole apartment."

Tyler poured himself a glass of milk and raised it in the air. "Thank you, Grandma May," he said.

~

That night, Mike barbecued chicken in the backyard. Lizzie sat on the porch, nervously watching the upstairs windows of the garage. Tyler knew not to turn on lights, not to make any noise, and not to stand near the windows where he could be seen. They'd closed the windows that faced the house, so from the yard, the apartment looked as still and empty as it always did.

"Hey, Mike?" Lizzie asked. She had her notebook open on her lap, casually sketching the tree house on its tall, delicate stilts. That was the other thing she liked about keeping a journal; there were no rules. If she wanted to cover one page with a drawing, or another with a poem, that was her choice. John Muir had made a lot of sketches in his journal, too.

Lizzie D.

John Muir's lost cabin
(Yosemite Creek or Tenaya Creek)

Her father seemed preoccupied, turning pieces of chicken over the smoldering coals.

Lizzie tried again. "Dad."

Now he looked up. "What?"

"There's an old picture in Grandma May's apartment, of a wooden house or something. In the woods. Do you know what that is?"

"Sure. It's John Muir's lost cabin."

Lizzie leaned forward. "What? John Muir had a cabin?"

He glanced up. "Yeah. In Yosemite. Don't you know about that? I thought you were studying him in school."

Lizzie held up her notebook. "We are. It's my homework for the summer, remember? Keeping this journal, like John Muir did."

Sometimes she felt like her father paid no attention to her life at all.

"Well, that's what I thought," he said, clearly trying to cover for his lapse. "Muir lived in Yosemite in the late 1800s, and he built a cabin by a stream. It was a mill, actually. A sawmill, with a little shack on top of it that he lived in. Lots of famous people visited him in Yosemite."

"Like who?" Lizzie asked.

"Let's see. Teddy Roosevelt went camping with

him . . . and he was the president who probably did the most for the national parks. And Ralph Waldo Emerson stayed with Muir once."

"Who's that?"

Mike sighed. "Emerson? Thoreau? Ring any bells?"

"Nope."

"Emerson was a great thinker and writer of the nineteenth century, part of the transcendentalist movement."

Lizzie rested her chin in her hands. She was starting to feel bored. "What's that? A religion?"

Her father thought for a minute. "It's kind of hard to explain, but basically Emerson and Thoreau and the other transcendentalists believed that people were fundamentally pure and good on their own, out in nature. But not in civilization."

Lizzie thought about that. Did people behave worse around other people than they did on their own? She wasn't so sure. She thought most people behaved better when someone else was watching.

"Did John Muir believe that?" she asked.

"I would bet so," her father said. "He thought nature was the source of beauty, and peace, and everything good, and he convinced a lot of other people that he was right."

"How'd he do that? Why did anyone listen to him?"

Her father thought for a minute. "Well, his ideas were new, you know? I mean, it's hard for you to see it now, because we recycle everything, and we conserve water, and we try to be so careful about the environment. But back in John Muir's time, nature was just seen as . . . well, a resource, something to be used up."

"What do you mean?" Lizzie asked.

Mike turned the chicken pieces with his tongs, and they sizzled over the flames.

"I'm trying to think how I can explain it to you," he said after a bit. "A long time ago, people were pretty much only interested in nature for what they could get from it. Land was for farming, animals were for eating, trees were for lumber, water was for irrigation. Coal, silver, gold—if anything could be taken out of the wilderness and used by humans, it was. John Muir was one of the first people who saw the danger of that . . . how it was destroying the wilderness."

"And that was a new idea?"

"Yes. Muir thought nature should be protected and preserved, because he knew once we used it up, we might never get it back. And through his writing—his letters, his books, his journals—he convinced people that wilderness should be preserved. That it had value all on its own, not just as something humans could use. And that really was a new idea."

Lizzie was silent for a minute. "Is that why the zoo is named for him?"

Mike smiled. "Well, this is kind of his territory. Around Yosemite, a lot of things are named for him."

Lizzie looked down at her sketch again. "But what about the lost cabin?"

"Yeah, the lost cabin. There's a picture of it in the apartment. Muir built it around the 1860s, supposedly somewhere along either Yosemite Creek or Tenaya Creek."

"Really? He lived there? It looks like a tree house. It's got different floors, and it's kind of on stilts." Lizzie smoothed the open page of her notebook with the drawing of the cabin and, below her picture, she wrote in small print, *John Muir's lost cabin. Yosemite Creek or Tenaya Creek.*

"That's because it was built near a waterfall," her father said. "As part of the mill."

"But why did you say it was a lost cabin?" Lizzie asked, losing patience.

"Because that's what it's called—John Muir's lost cabin. Nobody's ever been able to find it."

A lost cabin! She couldn't wait to tell Tyler. "How come?"

"Well, you saw the picture. It doesn't look too sturdy. It probably fell apart or got destroyed a long time ago. Maybe it was washed away in the creek. And nobody's even sure exactly where it was located. Your mom and I—" Mike stopped.

"What?" Lizzie set her notebook on the step and leaned forward, hugging her knees. She loved hearing stories about her mother.

"Your mom and I used to go on camping trips in Yosemite to look for it."

"You did?" It was the first Lizzie had heard of this, though she knew that her parents had loved camping in Yosemite before she was born. She liked this new image, of her young mother and father exploring the park, searching for a lost cabin.

"Yosemite Creek, by the falls, is such a tourist attraction, it definitely would have been discovered if it were still there. But Tenaya Creek goes through Tenaya Canyon, and that part of the park is pretty much off-limits."

"What do you mean, off-limits?" Lizzie asked.

"Well, it's really rough terrain, very steep in parts, with lots of waterfalls. The park rangers discourage people from hiking or camping there. There have been injuries and deaths in the canyon. And then there's Chief Tenaya's curse."

A curse! Lizzie picked up her notebook again, thinking she should write this down. "What's the curse?"

"Just an old superstition," her father said. "But based on something real, the way legends usually are. Chief Tenaya was the leader of the Ahwahneechee tribe in Yosemite Valley. When the white settlers tried to move the Indians to a reservation, his son was killed, and then the chief cursed forever after any white person who dared to set foot in Tenaya Canyon."

Forever after? Lizzie shivered. It sounded like a fairy tale. "So white people who go into the canyon will die?" She jotted the curse down in her notebook, near the picture of the lost cabin.

"It's a dangerous place," her father said. "Hikers get lost, injured, or killed in Yosemite every year, and many of those incidents happen in Tenaya Canyon. It's one of the few places in Yosemite where John Muir himself had a fall."

"Really? And you and Mom hiked there?" Lizzie asked in surprise.

"No, no," her father said quickly. "We're not mountaineers! We didn't have climbing equipment. But we hiked a good stretch of Tenaya Creek, and then turned back when the trail ended. We never saw any sign of the cabin."

Mike stared at the glowing coals. "She loved that photo of your grandmother's because it belonged to Clare Hodges."

He lapsed into silence, and Lizzie could tell he was sad. Sometimes talking about her mother made him happy, but other times, it seemed to suck the light out of him. She wished she could take back the barrage of questions that had ended up leading them here.

To change the subject, she said, "How was your day?"

Her father always had interesting stories from work, either about animal exploits or human ones. Sometimes the behavior of the people at the zoo was far stranger than that of the animals.

Mike used the tongs to move a piece of chicken away from the grill's orange flames. "Athena has gotten worse," he said. "Karen doesn't think she's going to make it."

"What?" Lizzie sprang to her feet, panicked. "But you said she would be okay."

"I know, honey. I thought she would be. But she got a lot sicker last night, apparently."

"Did you go check on her?"

"I didn't have a chance today, and Karen is worried about containing the illness, in case it's contagious." He hesitated. "One of the other wolves doesn't look so good now."

Lizzie's heart clenched. "It's *not Lobo*, is it?"

"No, no, he seems fine." Mike rearranged the pieces of chicken over the coals. "It's the other young female, Tamarack. She's . . . well, hopefully it's nothing. I thought she seemed lethargic when I stopped by this afternoon, and I saw her vomit."

Lizzie knew that "lethargic" described an animal that wasn't up to its usual level of energy or activity. "Are you giving her medicine? What are you doing to help her get better?" she asked urgently.

"It's hard to treat it when we don't know what it is," Mike said. "Sometimes these things just have to run their course. Karen has Ed keeping an eye on her." Ed was Karen's assistant in the clinic, a thin, bearded graduate student who had barely spoken a word to Lizzie since he arrived at the zoo a year ago.

Just then, her father's cell phone rang, shattering the evening quiet.

Mike set down the tongs and fished his phone out of his pocket. "Hello? Oh, hi, Karen. What?" He tensed. "She did? Oh."

He stood silent, listening. Lizzie could tell from his expression that something bad had happened.

"Okay, well, I'll come right over." He paused. "Oh, you did?" Mike grimaced. "Already?"

The chicken sizzled and popped, and he turned back to the grill. "Shoot! No, I'm just burning something over here. Yeah, okay, we'll talk tomorrow. Thanks, Karen. I know that wasn't easy."

He clicked the phone off and turned to Lizzie. "She had to put Athena down."

Lizzie covered her face with her hands. Even though Athena was one of the shyest wolves, she could picture her clearly. She was slim, more delicate than the others, and a tawny brown color.

"What happened?"

Mike piled the crispy chicken on a platter. "She couldn't walk and her legs were spasming. Karen said she was having trouble breathing."

"But what was it? What made her sick?"

Mike ran his hand through his hair, his face grim. "We're hoping it's an isolated thing. I was thinking we should do an autopsy . . ."

Lizzie flinched at the word, which sounded both hopeless and final.

"But Karen's already disposed of the carcass," he continued grimly. "She's trying to contain it, whatever it is that killed her."

He lowered the lid of the grill and climbed the steps to the back door. "Come inside, Lizzie. We might as well eat."

She didn't feel at all hungry. They sat at the table in silence, picking at their dinner, as the clock over the kitchen stove ticked loudly.

After a while, Lizzie said, "Athena was one of the youngest ones, wasn't she?"

Mike nodded. "About three years old." He stood, scraping their plates into the garbage and knotting the bag. "I feel really bad about it."

"Me too," Lizzie said.

And then she stiffened, realizing that her father must be planning to take the garbage out to the garage. She jumped up. "I can take that out if you want."

Mike looked surprised, but then nodded. "Okay. I'll

 101

go upstairs and e-mail the board. I should let them know about Athena. We haven't lost an animal in a couple of years."

Lizzie noticed the slump of his shoulders as he left the kitchen. Anything that happened to the animals, her father took personally. It was what made him a good zookeeper, Lizzie knew, but it also meant he would feel responsible for this and worry about it.

When she was sure he was upstairs on the computer, she quickly assembled a plate of food for Tyler—some chicken, potato salad, coleslaw, and a hard roll. She covered it with foil and, juggling the bulky garbage bag in her other hand, she slipped out the side door to the garage.

After she'd dumped the bag in the trash can she took the key out from under the flowerpot and let herself into the apartment. Tyler was waiting for her at the top of the stairs.

"I'm starving!" he said. "I could smell that chicken all the way up here."

Lizzie had been excited to tell him about the lost cabin, but now she didn't feel like talking. She handed him the plate and turned to go.

"What's the matter?" he asked.

"One of the wolves died."

His eyes widened. "No . . . for real?"

"Yeah."

"Oh." He put the plate on the table, glancing at it, and she could tell how eager he was to rip off the foil and start eating. But he waited. "Was it sick?"

"Yeah."

Tyler hesitated. "Well, you know, it probably lived longer here in the zoo than it would've in the wild."

"Maybe. But it was one of the young ones."

Tyler was quiet for a minute, watching her. Finally, he said, "The animals here, they got so many people to take care of them . . . your dad, and the vet, and the other zookeepers. If that wolf died here, I just think it would have died anywhere. You know? Probably nothing anybody could do."

Lizzie sighed. She knew he was trying to make her feel better. "I guess you're right." She took a deep breath. "But my dad says one of the other wolves looked sick today."

"Oh," Tyler said. "You think it's something catching?"

Lizzie nodded. "I go to Wolf Woods every day, and I saw a couple of them lying down this morning. But they were in the back of the pen, not close enough for me to see if anything was wrong."

"Hey." Tyler brightened. "We could go there tonight if you want. To check on them. Want to? Would that make you feel better?"

Lizzie looked at him in surprise. "Now? It's dark out." She peered through the apartment windows into the yard, which was a blur of shapes and textures in the soft moonlight.

"We'll take a flashlight."

Lizzie hesitated. "I'd have to wait till my dad is in bed."

"Sure." Tyler flashed a wide grin. "It's not like I've got somewhere to go."

"Okay," Lizzie decided. "Let's do it. I think it would make me feel better."

"Cool. When?"

"I'll come back in a couple of hours."

Tyler nodded. "I'll be ready."

She turned to leave.

"Lizzie?"

She smiled at him, warmed by the way he said her name.

"Yeah?"

He was still standing at the table, and she knew it must be taking every ounce of his self-control not to start eating. "Thanks for dinner."

"Sure."

"And for letting me stay here."

Lizzie nodded. "No problem. Better than the elephant house, right?"

"Yeah. A lot better."

"See? Told you."

Chapter 10

A NIGHT VISITOR

THAT NIGHT, AS soon as Mike's breathing turned heavy and slow in the next room, Lizzie got dressed and grabbed a flashlight from the kitchen drawer. She opened the back door quietly and stepped into the dark yard, sending one guilty glance at her father's darkened window. Going into the zoo at night felt no different from walking around her own yard—it was so familiar to her. Still, if Mike woke up for some reason and found her gone, he would be worried. Tyler was sitting on the stoop outside the garage. She jumped when she saw him shifting in the blackness.

"What are you doing out here? Somebody might see you!"

"I was feeling cooped up," he said. "I'm not used to being inside so much. And anyway, it's dark now. Nobody can see me. I blend in a lot better than you do."

That was true, Lizzie thought, and it had probably been an advantage during the nights he was hiding out at the elephant house. Together they started up the moonlit driveway, heading into the zoo. The night air was crisp, thrumming with strange noises. Lizzie heard the trilling of insects, sometimes the distant snort or chirp of one of the zoo animals. The banks of flowers along the walk, so bright during the day, became ghostly shadows at night.

Lizzie shone the flashlight in an arc in front of them, and they hurried down the walkway toward Wolf Woods. "We have to watch out for the security guard. Sometimes he leaves his booth and takes a walk around."

"Believe me, I know," Tyler said.

Lizzie thought of all the nights he'd spent here alone. "Weren't you scared?" she asked. "Sleeping outside, all by yourself?"

"Nah," Tyler scoffed. "I like being on my own."

"Oh, I almost forgot!" Lizzie grabbed his arm. "I asked my dad about that old picture of the cabin. Turns out it's John Muir's lost cabin!"

"Huh?" Tyler looked at her blankly. "Muir, like the guy the zoo is named for?"

"Yes," Lizzie said. With her words tumbling over each other, she quickly explained about John Muir, Yosemite, the cursed canyon, and the lost cabin.

"And nobody's been able to find it?" he asked when she was finished, his eyes bright with excitement.

"Nope! It's been lost for a hundred years. Maybe more. We should look up when John Muir died."

"So you think it's still up in the mountains somewhere? In Yosemite?"

"I don't know. But it would be fun to try to find it. Except if it's really in Tenaya Canyon, it sounds like nobody can get to it."

"Maybe that's why it's never been found," Tyler said thoughtfully. "We should go there sometime."

Yosemite was an hour's drive away. Lizzie wondered how they could ever do that. "My dad would take us," she said. "But we'd have to tell him about you."

Tyler grimaced. "We can't do that."

"Well, we could say you're a friend of mine," Lizzie suggested.

He shook his head. "You know what would happen then. He'd be all, 'Where do you live?' and 'I have to ask your parents.'"

"Yeah, maybe," Lizzie said. "But I don't know how else we could get into the park. It's pretty far away. Have you ever been?"

Tyler shook his head. "No. But it sounds cool."

Lizzie had been to Yosemite many times with her father and twice with her grandmother, not usually in the summer, when it was crowded, but in the fall, when many of the trails were empty. The park was so vast, she'd only seen a fraction of it, but she thought it was one of the most beautiful, magical spots on earth, with its high rocky cliffs and rushing, misty waterfalls. She'd spotted a black bear once, lumbering idly through the woods, and it had made her never want to see a bear in a zoo cage again.

"We should try to go," Lizzie told him. "Because you would love it."

When they got to Wolf Woods, there was no sign of the wolves in the dark enclosure.

"They must be back there by the trees," Lizzie said, sweeping the flashlight across the pen.

Tyler started to climb over the guardrail. "Let's walk on the side, along the fence."

Lizzie hesitated. "There isn't a path. It's all bushes. I've never gone all the way back there."

"Well, how else are we going to check on the wolves?" Tyler demanded. "They're too far away. We can't see anything from here."

Lizzie eyed the dark thicket of bushes crowding close to the fence. "I guess we can try."

Together, they scrambled over the guardrail into the brush. "Here, give me the flashlight," Tyler ordered. "I'll go first."

"I think I should go first," Lizzie said. "I know the way."

"You just said you'd never been back here." Tyler took the flashlight from her. "And anyway, I'm used to walking around this place after dark. You're not."

Lizzie frowned at the back of his head as he pushed past her. "Don't boss me around," she said.

"Come on, I can see them now." He crashed through the bushes a few yards ahead of her.

"Keep it down," Lizzie warned. "You'll scare them."

Now she, too, could see the wolves. They must have been lying down, but at the burst of noise coming from outside the fence, they immediately rose to their feet . . . all except one, a pale silver wolf whose fur was almost white.

"I think that's Tamarack," Lizzie whispered, pointing.

Tyler directed his flashlight toward the pack, and the wolves began pacing in agitation, ears pricked, faces turned toward Lizzie and Tyler. She could see Lobo's dim silhouette, larger than the rest. He walked toward them, his ghostly eyes glowing in the beam of light.

"That's Lobo," she told Tyler.

"Wow," Tyler said. "He's a big guy. I wouldn't want to run into him in the woods."

"I know," Lizzie agreed. "He's the pack leader."

Lobo lifted his nose and sniffed the air. Lizzie thought she could see his hackles rise. Suddenly his head swung around in the opposite direction, and in unison, the other wolves stopped pacing and looked that way, too. They were gazing toward the back of the pen, away from Tyler and Lizzie.

Lizzie heard something in the rear of the enclosure, noises that seemed to be coming from the building. Instinctively, she grabbed the flashlight and switched it off. "Shhhh," she whispered to Tyler. "I think someone's here."

"I told you," Tyler said. "I've seen somebody here at night before."

"What would they be doing? It's too dark to see anything." Lobo trotted toward the back of the pen. All of the other wolves—except for the one lying down—

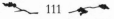

followed him. Lizzie strained to hear anything over the night noises of the zoo. She thought she heard the click of something being unlatched.

"What's going on?" Tyler whispered.

"I don't know."

"Where did the wolves go?"

Lizzie scanned the enclosure. Except for Tamarack, who was still lying on the ground, the wolves seemed to have disappeared. She didn't see them anywhere.

She turned to Tyler in bewilderment. "There's a little fenced yard behind the pen. My dad uses that to separate the wolves sometimes, or to feed them. I think they went in there . . . but someone must have opened the gate." She kept staring through the fence, across the dark field. It didn't make sense. Who would have opened the back gate at night?

"Wait," she said suddenly. "Get down."

She dropped to her knees and pulled Tyler with her.

"What's the matter?" Tyler whispered.

"Somebody's in the pen. See?"

Leaves scratched their faces and nearly blocked their view. They huddled silently, pressed against the wire mesh of the fence.

A blurry human silhouette was walking across the

pen toward Tamarack, who was still lying on the ground. The sick wolf began to move, struggling to get up, but her hind legs sagged uselessly. The human shape crouched quickly, and Lizzie saw a hand reach out toward the wolf's flank. Then the wolf fell back down, and after a minute, the blurred silhouette stood and walked toward the back of the pen.

A series of muffled noises drifted through the night air. Suddenly, the other wolves came trotting back into the field. There was no sign of Lobo.

Lizzie tensed. "Where's Lobo? He's always in the lead."

They heard more rustling at the back of the pen, and then Lobo appeared, streaking across the dark enclosure. What had he been doing back there?

"What's happening?" Tyler asked, his voice hushed.

"I don't know," Lizzie said.

After a few minutes, a motor rumbled, and they could hear the crunch of gravel under tires.

"That's a car," Tyler said. "Somebody drove here."

Lizzie nodded. "They must have come on the access road and gotten into the pen from the back." She listened for a minute. "They're gone. Let's walk down there and take a look."

Carefully, with the flashlight still turned off, they picked their way through the bushes toward the rear of the pen, where the wolves were gathered in a nervous cluster, looking alert. Lizzie could see that Lobo was standing over the wolf on the ground, sniffing her.

As they approached, the other wolves scattered to the opposite side of the enclosure. Lobo stayed where he was, watching Lizzie and Tyler.

Now they were next to the fence, only a few yards from the two wolves.

Even in the darkness, Lizzie could see Lobo's head lower slightly, and the fur on his shoulders stiffen.

Tyler took the flashlight. "Can I turn it on?"

"Yeah, I think so."

The area of the pen right in front of them was suddenly awash in light. Lobo began to pace back and forth only a few yards away, ears pricked, ruff raised. Lizzie could feel his silvery eyes boring through her.

The wolf on the ground was clearly sick. It was Tamarack, the other young female—Lizzie recognized her white form immediately in the circle of light. She lay flat, her legs trembling. She did not lift her head or try to stand. Lizzie felt a hopeless pit expand in her stomach.

"That one doesn't look good," Tyler said.

Lobo, meanwhile, had stopped pacing. He stood

frozen in the light, his head down, tail flat, lips curling over the glint of teeth.

Lizzie had never seen him like that, but she knew instinctively what was coming. "Oh no," she whispered. "He's going to attack!"

Chapter 11

LOBO

BEFORE THEY HAD time to react, the big wolf leapt through the air, teeth bared, his enormous form flying straight at them. He crashed into the fence, jaws snapping.

For an instant, Lizzie could smell him and feel him, the wildness of him, the closeness of his gaping mouth.

"Watch out!" Tyler cried. He stumbled backward, grabbing Lizzie's arm. They fell into the brambles, and the flashlight rolled away from Tyler into the dark bushes. Inside the pen, they could see Lobo pacing next to the fence, his ruff still spiked, his ears pressed to his skull.

Lizzie crawled on her hands and knees to the flashlight. Fingers trembling, she fumbled to turn off the beam. "Let's get out of here," she whispered.

"Yeah, no kidding," Tyler answered. "If that fence wasn't there, we'd be dead right now."

"I know." Lizzie's voice caught. "I've never seen him like that. Come on."

Without the help of the flashlight, they careened through the brush, tripping over roots and rocks, scratching their bare legs. It wasn't until they'd hopped back over the guardrail that Lizzie felt able to take a breath. She collapsed on the big rock where she had sat so often to write in her notebook.

"Man, what was that?" Tyler asked, pacing in front of her, as agitated as the wolves.

Lizzie shook her head. "I guess we freaked him out, coming so close."

"But he didn't even growl at us! He just jumped."

Lizzie nodded. "That's what they do. My dad says you don't have to worry when they're making noise. It's when they're silent that they might attack you."

"Why would he attack us?" Tyler demanded. "We weren't doing anything."

"I don't know," she said, breathing deeply and trying to still her quaking knees.

"Maybe he was protecting the sick one," Tyler suggested.

"Tamarack? Yeah, maybe." Lizzie bit her lip. "She looked really bad. She couldn't stand."

The possibility that another of the wolves might be close to death was too much for her to contemplate. If it was a contagious illness, they were all at risk. Even Lobo.

Tyler walked back and forth along the curb, shaking his head. "Who was that inside the pen?"

Lizzie shook her head. "I don't know. I couldn't see."

"But how did they get in? I mean, aren't all the cages locked?"

"Yes, of course."

"Well, who has the key to Wolf Woods?"

Lizzie looked at him, stricken. "Only the zookeepers, I think. It doesn't make sense."

"Maybe somebody broke in," Tyler suggested.

"Yeah," Lizzie said. "But did you see them bend down by Tamarack? Whoever it was did something to her."

"Maybe someone was giving her medicine."

"Maybe," Lizzie said doubtfully. "But why would anybody do that at night? My dad never goes into the cages with the dangerous animals alone. It's against the rules. Even the ones you've known forever can turn on you. Look at Lobo tonight. My dad says, 'You take the wolf out of the wild, but you can't take the wild out of the wolf.'"

Tyler nodded. "He got scared. Or mad."

They looked at each other in the dark.

"Something is going on," Tyler said.

Lizzie turned back to the wolves, shrouded in darkness under the pines. "I'm worried about them."

"We should get out of here," Tyler told her.

In silence, with the flashlight still off, they followed the path back to Lizzie's house.

The next morning, Lizzie dragged her exhausted self down to the kitchen table and tried to pretend she'd gotten more than a few hours of sleep. Going to bed so late was bad enough, but she'd had tortured dreams in which she was lost in the woods, being chased by wolves. She'd been utterly alone.

As Mike drank his coffee, Lizzie's mind raced with questions from the night before. "Dad," she said, "do the keepers ever go into the cages at night?"

He shook his head. "Only in an emergency."

"What's an emergency?"

Mike thought for a minute. "Well, anything where the animals are at risk. Do you remember that big storm a few years ago? The tree that fell over in the African Savannah? It shorted out the fence, and Wesley and I had to go in there at night to fix it."

Lizzie did vaguely remember that . . . the loud, crashing storm, and being awakened in the middle of the night because her father was heading out to deal with a crisis. "So the custodians can go inside the cages, too?"

"Well, yes, but that's very rare."

"What about the keepers' assistants?" Lizzie persisted. "People like Ed. Do they have keys?"

Mike was looking at her over the rim of his mug. "Why are you asking?"

 120

Lizzie tried to act nonchalant. "I just wondered." She poured cereal into a bowl and tried a different tack. "Are animals ever taken out of the zoo? If they're sick?"

"You mean like Athena? Not usually. We have an operating room in the clinic, and if we ever had a medical problem that Karen couldn't handle, we'd call in another zoo vet, someone from San Diego. There are a bunch of permissions needed to transport zoo animals . . . even if it's just to another zoo to breed them."

"But what if Tamarack has the same thing as Athena? Will you call in another vet?"

"It depends on what's wrong. If it's a virus . . ." Mike was quiet, his brow furrowed. "Well, it's unlikely anyone will be able to do anything. The most important thing is to contain it. We're going to move Tamarack to the clinic today."

Lizzie's heart sank. "Do you think she's going to die?"

"I don't know, honey. Whatever it is, it's serious. I'm just praying the rest of the pack stays healthy."

"Can I come? When you take her to the clinic? Please, Dad."

Mike hesitated.

He never allowed her to have contact with animals that were sick or had behavior problems. But these were the wolves! She'd spent the whole summer getting to know them. She looked at him beseechingly. "I won't get in the way, I promise. It's just that . . ."

He sighed and stood up, ruffling her hair as he passed by. "I know. You've gotten attached to the wolves. I have, too. Okay, I guess you can come. But you'll have to do what Karen says, and you can't touch Tamarack. Understand?"

"I won't," Lizzie promised.

SICK WOLF

LIZZIE WAS DYING to tell Tyler what she was doing, but there was no way to talk to him before she left the house. She would have to report back later. She glanced up at the blank face of the upper windows of the apartment as she and her father walked down the driveway. There was no sign of activity, thank goodness, and she was relieved they'd remembered to close the windows that were visible from the yard. Tyler appeared to be good at lying low—not surprising, Lizzie thought, given the time he'd spent in hiding. She wondered about his foster family. However bad it had been for him, they were probably crazy with worry now, not knowing where he was. And what about his real mother and father? She remembered what he'd said: "Everything that happened to them, they did to themselves." What did that mean?

She walked alongside her father through the morning stillness of the zoo. The gates wouldn't open for another hour. They passed one of the custodians, Joe Walsh, emptying a trash bin. Lizzie waved at him.

"Hey, Joe," Mike called.

"Hey, Mike. I see you brought reinforcements," he said, gesturing at Lizzie.

Mike grinned. "Always good to have backup." He glanced down at her. "We'll go to the clinic first," he said as they walked. "I told Karen I'd meet her there. But remember not to touch anything, okay?"

Lizzie nodded. She knew Karen was fussy about the clinic. Nobody was allowed in there except for her assistants and occasionally one of the keepers. Lizzie herself had only been in the front office, never inside the medical treatment area.

They passed the crocodile moat. Both of the crocs lay in the morning sunlight, so still they might have been sleeping, except that their small, glittering eyes were open. Lizzie knew they needed to warm up before they were able to move.

A chain-link fence bordered the crocodile moat, and behind it was the vet's clinic, the one-story gray building where Karen worked. Mike fumbled with his ring of keys at the gate, but before he had time to fit one into the lock, Karen came down the steps of the clinic, in her usual beige coveralls, blond ponytail swinging.

"I'll get it," she called, striding across the dusty yard and opening the gate for them. "Hi, Lizzie. What are you up to?"

"I came to help," Lizzie said, suddenly shy. "With Tamarack."

"Oh." Karen glanced at Mike, and Lizzie felt embarrassed.

"She won't get in our way," Mike said.

Lizzie's cheeks grew hot. Of course she wouldn't get in their way! She'd been helping with animals at the zoo her whole life.

Karen pursed her lips, then seemed to relent. "Okay, that's fine. Just don't touch anything, Lizzie. Whatever it is, it's contagious."

"I know," Lizzie said. "I'll be careful."

Karen gestured to a metal sink against the wall of the clinic, with a clear plastic dispenser full of pink foaming soap mounted near it. "Wash your hands. We'll take the truck. Ed is meeting us there."

Lizzie stiffened. Had Ed been the one in the wolf pen last night?

She and Mike silently scrubbed their hands under a stream of hot water while Karen waited. Her big white truck was parked next to the clinic, and when they all climbed into it, Lizzie saw that there was a large metal cage in the back.

"How will you get Tamarack in there?" she asked. Last night, the wolf hadn't seemed strong enough to even stand, but she wasn't in a position to tell Karen how she knew that.

"She's pretty weak," Karen acknowledged, "but you'd be surprised how quickly they rally when they're scared. If we can't get her to her feet and herd her in, we'll carry her."

"Have you or Ed been over there this morning?" Mike asked. "How are the others looking?"

Karen nodded. "I went first thing. The rest of the pack seems fine. Lobo knows something is up. He's being protective, so watch out."

Lizzie thought of last night, when Lobo had lunged at them in the darkness . . . the terrifying bulk of him, the menacing glimmer of his teeth. She shuddered.

"You okay?" her father asked.

"Yes," she said, steeling herself. "It's just cool this morning."

"It won't be in another couple of hours," Karen said. "Temps in the nineties today."

She turned the key in the ignition and the truck engine roared. They drove along the gravel access road behind the main exhibit houses, then through the pine grove that bordered Wolf Woods. Karen drove the way she did everything else, Lizzie thought—with a quick, impatient confidence. She knew from Mike that years ago, Karen had worked for something called Nature Justice, an environmental organization that fought to protect various animals and habitats from human destruction, sometimes by breaking the law. Mike jokingly called her a "radical" because of her views—but Karen was nothing like the fiery, violent protesters Lizzie pictured when he said that. Still, it was easy to imagine Karen staying calm in dangerous situations. She always seemed so sure of what she was doing. She was cool and quiet and careful; hard to get to know, in Lizzie's experience, and though Mike never talked about it, she suspected he thought the same. Even though he and Karen had gone out a few times, they didn't exactly seem close. The thing they had in common was their total devotion to the animals.

As they drove up to Wolf Woods, Lizzie scanned the area. Who had been back here the night before? The only way to get there by vehicle was via the access road, which was entirely on zoo property. It didn't connect to the Lodisto town roads.

The wolf exhibit consisted of the two-acre enclosure; the concrete building with cages, a small kitchen, and examination room; and a smaller fenced pen adjacent to the building, which was called a secondary containment area. All of the enclosures had one; by zoo regulations, any gate or door opening out of an animal pen had to lead to a second pen, so that if the first gate failed, there was a second barrier that prevented the animals from running loose.

Karen swiftly backed up the truck to within a few feet of the wolf building. Lizzie knew this was so she could easily move Tamarack from the building to the truck, minimizing time in the open.

"Get the cage ready," Karen said, switching off the engine and hopping out.

Mike climbed down and released the tailgate of the truck, which dropped with a clang. Then he unlatched the door to the cage.

"Wait here," he told Lizzie. "We'll separate the rest of the pack so we can get to Tamarack."

"Can I help?" Lizzie asked.

"Not with this part. Just give us a few minutes."

Quietly, Lizzie climbed out of the truck and wandered closer to the fence.

Along one side of the smaller fenced yard was a metal trough, a feeding station. The wolves, hearing activity behind the building, were now gathered within view, pacing nervously, watching Karen and Mike. Lizzie counted four, and then saw Lobo standing at a distance from the others. That made five. Tamarack was lying down somewhere . . . which made six . . . and Athena was gone. Lizzie thought of all the times during the summer that she had watched and counted the pack of seven. What if Tamarack died, too? She couldn't bear to think about it.

"Ed's here with the blow darts," Karen said as she and Mike disappeared inside the building. The keepers carried blow pipes into the cages so they could immediately tranquilize an animal that threatened them. But in the case of the wolves, the thought still made Lizzie nervous. A blow dart didn't seem like much protection against a wolf as big as Lobo.

The wolves circled by the gate that opened into the small yard. Like all the zoo animals, they knew the keepers' routines. There was food in the building. Lizzie saw that only Lobo held back, but he too seemed agitated.

Karen emerged into the little yard with two packages of hamburger meat, which she unwrapped and dumped into the trough, pulling the meat apart with her hands and spreading it along the bottom of the metal bin. The wolves were even more excited now, trotting back and forth on the other side of the fence. Mike stood ready to unlock the inner gate into the wolf enclosure.

Lizzie had seen her father enter animal compounds many, many times, but it always struck her anew what a complicated procedure it was. The goal was always to keep the zookeepers or animal handlers separate and safe from the animals . . . especially predators. But that could be difficult when some kind of direct interaction was necessary—for instance, with a sick animal, like Tamarack.

Karen waited in the doorway of the wolf building with a large blanket under one arm and a blue plastic bag in her hand. With her was the lanky graduate student, Ed. Lizzie watched him suspiciously.

"What about Lobo?" Mike asked. "He's staying away."

"I have a piece of steak for him," Karen said, holding up the blue bag. "But we may have to tranquilize him."

"Why?" Lizzie cried. She had assumed the blow dart was meant for Tamarack.

"If he interferes," Karen said.

"Okay, ready?" Mike asked.

"Yep," Karen said.

They all disappeared into the wolf building and a minute later, the metal gate to the small yard opened.

Four of the wolves rushed in. They scrambled over one another to get to the trough, and in a fit of growling and whining, began to devour the meat. Lizzie could hear the wet, greedy sounds of them gulping it down, then the clicks of their teeth against the empty food bin.

She could see that Lobo was keeping his distance, watching the others.

A minute later, from the safety of the building, Mike closed the gate, separating the four wolves from Lobo and Tamarack, who remained in the large pen.

Lizzie hurried around the side of the building to have a better view of Lobo and Tamarack. She immediately saw Tamarack's white form lying in the dirt, her legs twitching. Lobo was trotting back and forth near her, his hackles raised.

Now Mike and Karen were going to have to enter the pen with Lobo still inside. Lizzie caught her breath. Ed stood in the doorway of the building with the blow pipe raised, dart ready.

"Give me the steak," Mike said to Karen in a low voice.

She handed him the bag, and Mike broke off from the other two, walking in the opposite direction, toward the far side of the enclosure. Lizzie saw that he had a blow pipe in his belt. "Lobo," he called.

The wolf stood still, sniffing the air.

Lizzie felt a thin, ice-cold prick of fear. There was nothing between the wolf and her father.

"Lobo," Mike called again. He tore off a piece of steak and tossed it to a spot about twenty yards from Lobo.

The wolf began to pace back and forth, his eyes glued on Mike, but he stayed near Tamarack.

Karen edged closer, with Ed behind her. The big wolf trotted in a tight circle around Tamarack, ears pricked forward, body tense.

Then he saw Lizzie approaching the fence. He stopped. His silver eyes fixed on her. Lizzie lifted her fingers and curled them around the chain link, staring back at him.

"Now!" Karen said softly.

Lizzie heard the soft, percussive sound of the blow dart. She covered her mouth in horror.

Lobo leapt forward, whether from the sound or the dart hitting him, Lizzie couldn't tell. Then he staggered.

A moment later, he collapsed on the ground. With that thud, Lizzie could feel the full weight of her betrayal.

Now Karen and Mike hurried over to Tamarack, who was struggling on the ground, trying to rise. She seemed unable to get her rear feet underneath her.

"Hurry," Karen said. "We may not have long before he's up again."

They spread the blanket next to Tamarack. Lizzie could see her writhing away from them. Within minutes they had muzzled her and moved her onto the blanket.

Then Ed and Mike carried her into the building, heaving the large, sagging bundle between them.

"Lizzie," Karen called. "Can you get the back door for them? I'm going to check on Lobo."

"Not on your own—" Mike started to warn, but Karen was already walking toward the spot where Lobo lay.

"Sure," Lizzie said as Mike yelled, "Lizzie! Open the back door!"

Lizzie ran around to the back of the building and opened the heavy door.

"Watch out," Mike said as he and Ed hoisted the blanketed bundle onto the tailgate of the truck, then into the cage. Tamarack thrashed and squirmed, snarling at them. Lizzie could see the wolf's wild, frightened eyes.

"She's still got some fight in her," Mike said. He pushed the cage toward the center of the big truck bed, then slammed the tailgate. "Maybe she's going to be okay."

"Really? Do you think so?" Lizzie asked.

But her father had already stepped back into the building. "Ed, is Karen in there alone?" he demanded.

Just then, Karen called to them from the other side of the small feeding yard, where the wolves had long since finished their meal and were circling nervously.

"Ed and I will come back to release the others," she said. "Let's get Tamarack out of here."

"Karen, what the heck?" Mike snapped. "You just violated about six AZA protocols. You'll get us all fired."

Lizzie looked at her father in surprise. It was rare that Mike lost his temper, but he sounded genuinely mad. She knew that nobody was supposed to be in the zoo enclosures alone, but Karen was the vet. If anyone should know how to handle the animals, it was Karen.

Karen seemed to be thinking the same thing, because she frowned at him. "Come on, help me close up."

Lizzie leaned over the side of the truck, watching Tamarack. She was lying quietly on the blanket inside the cage, but her legs twitched and jerked, and her eyes had a panicked look. What was wrong with her? *Please be all right,* Lizzie thought.

Chapter 13

A HIDDEN PICTURE

WHEN THEY GOT back to the clinic, Lizzie wanted to help unload Tamarack, but she could tell that none of the grown-ups were in the mood to be tolerant. Her father was still annoyed about the breach of rules; Karen was preoccupied with the sick wolf; and Ed immediately busied himself disinfecting the examination room before Tamarack was transferred out of the cage.

Mike lowered the tailgate. "I think we should call Dave Minowski in San Diego," he said. "They have a gray wolf there. Maybe he knows something about this illness."

"I already talked to him," Karen said, her voice curt. "I've got a call in to Woodland Park in Seattle."

Lizzie touched Mike's elbow. "I'm going back to the house," she said.

He barely glanced at her. "Okay, see you later."

She left them still arguing over what to do next.

As she walked up her driveway, Lizzie scanned the apartment windows and saw the curtains rustle behind one of them. Tyler greeted her at the bottom of the stairs, yanking the door open.

"What are you doing?" she demanded. "I could see the curtains moving! You have to be more careful."

"Whoa, take it easy," he said. "I saw it was just you. Besides, you said nobody comes back here during the day."

"Still," Lizzie chided. "You're not supposed to be looking out the windows at all."

"I got bored!" he protested. "I mean, don't get me wrong, I slept late in that puffy bed. It's, like, the best bed I ever slept in! But then you didn't come over. What happened?"

Lizzie followed him up the stairs into the sunny

apartment. "We moved Tamarack to the clinic. She seems really sick."

"Well, are they doing anything about it? Did they give her medicine?" Tyler asked, flopping on the couch.

Lizzie shrugged miserably. "I'm not sure. I don't think anyone knows what's wrong with her, so they're trying to figure out how to treat it. The vet, Karen, was talking to my dad about calling other zoos for help."

Tyler looked dissatisfied. "They should do a blood test or something."

Lizzie rolled her eyes at him.

"Well, at least I have some ideas. If another wolf dies, that would be, like, a third of them gone."

Lizzie sighed. "I know."

Tyler bounced up from the couch. "Hey! I have something to show you." He opened the bottom cupboard of the bookcase and took out a faded blue folder.

"What are you doing poking around in there?" Lizzie asked, startled. "That's Grandma May's stuff."

"Nah, it's nothing of hers," Tyler answered.

"How can you be sure? You shouldn't be looking at things that don't belong to you."

Tyler seemed genuinely puzzled. "If that's the rule, then I can't look at anything. Nothing belongs to me."

Lizzie started to contradict him; he had his backpack and clothing, didn't he? But, she realized, if those were his only possessions, they didn't amount to much. And she suspected they came from his foster family, so they probably didn't really feel like his, either.

"Don't you want to see what I found?" Tyler asked impatiently.

"Okay," she relented. They sat on the floor and Tyler opened the blue folder between them. There were some old, yellowed newspaper clippings—little articles about Yosemite, mostly—and some letters written in swirly, dense cursive, with drops of dark ink spotting the pages. Lizzie could barely decipher the words.

"Who are they from?" she asked.

"Clare Hodges! The park ranger. To your Grandma May," Tyler said triumphantly. "See how they're signed CMH? Remember how you said her middle name was Marie?"

Lizzie was impressed that he remembered that. "They must be old, then," she said. "What do they say?"

"I don't know," Tyler admitted. "They're really hard to read. But that's not even the best part." He shuffled through the file of letters and clippings until he came to a fragile photograph that was a soft brown color. It was a picture of two women standing near a stream, with a dense forest rising around them.

Lizzie lifted it carefully and held it in the sunlight, squinting at the image. "This looks like . . ."

Tyler nodded. "It is! It's the park ranger lady again, same as in the other picture." He scrambled to his feet and took the framed photograph from the bookshelf. "See?"

Lizzie saw that, indeed, the dark-haired, serious-faced young woman by the stream was the same as the one on the horse, though she looked younger in the picture by the creek.

"You're right," she said. "I wonder who the other woman is." The other woman was smaller-boned and older, with curly hair, a high-necked, frilly blouse, and a long dark skirt. She didn't look like she was dressed for a sojourn in the wilderness, which made the picture seem even odder.

"Who knows," Tyler said. "It doesn't say on the picture, but there's a date on the back . . . 1916. That's a hundred years ago!"

"Wow," Lizzie said. "I wonder if Grandma May remembers anything about this."

"Look closer," Tyler insisted, taking the sepia-toned photo and waving it under Lizzie's nose. "Do you see anything else interesting?"

Lizzie scanned the faded image. Mostly she saw the two women standing in front of a stream, and the wilderness crowding close. But when she peered at it more closely, she *did* see something else . . . some kind of structure on the far right side of the photo, half hidden by vegetation.

"What is it?" she asked Tyler, touching it lightly with her fingertip.

"Don't you know?" he asked.

Lizzie stared harder. It appeared to have more than one level, with a pointy little roof at the top. "Wait," she said slowly. "Is it . . . ?"

Her eyes grew wide.

"Yes!" Tyler cried jubilantly. "It's John Muir's lost cabin."

FAMILY HISTORY

"SO CLARE HODGES knew where it was? And went there?" Lizzie asked in amazement. "Into that canyon with the curse on it? She found the lost cabin!"

"It sure looks like it," Tyler said. "Do you think she ever told your grandma about it?"

"I don't know. Let's call her and find out."

Tyler sat back, his brow furrowing. "What, now? You can just call her and she'll answer?"

"Sure," Lizzie said. "I mean, she may not be there. She's pretty busy, and she has her bridge group today, I think. But let's see."

Lizzie took the phone from its wall-mount in the

kitchen and sat on the couch with her legs curled under her. She punched her grandmother's number.

Grandma May picked up on the third ring.

"Lizzie!" she said happily. "It's nice to hear your sweet voice. How is your summer going without Margaret?"

"Pretty well, actually," Lizzie said, and she realized to her surprise that she hadn't been missing Margaret as much as she'd feared. And then, because she felt disloyal, she added, "But I'll be really glad when she gets back from Australia."

Tyler whispered, "Who's Margaret?"

"My best friend," Lizzie explained softly, with her hand over the mouthpiece. She thought he looked annoyed, though whether it was about Margaret or how long it was taking to get to the point of the phone call, she couldn't be sure.

"Grandma? Do you mind if I put you on speaker?"

"Not at all," Grandma May answered. "I do that to you all the time." Her grandmother claimed that she could hear Lizzie better through the speakerphone, though Lizzie herself thought it made the conversation more halting and awkward. But she wanted Tyler to be able to hear what Grandma May said and she couldn't think of any other way to accomplish that, so she clicked

 144

the speaker button and set the phone faceup between them on the couch.

"I'm up in the apartment," Lizzie began.

"Getting ready for my visit?" Grandma May asked. "I can't wait to see you! And your father. Just a couple of weeks now."

"I know! I can't wait, either," Lizzie told her truthfully. "But I wanted to ask you about some pictures I found. You know that photo of your cousin Clare Hodges?"

"She's your cousin, too," Grandma May replied. "And yes, of course, I know it—the one on horseback? She was an extraordinary horsewoman."

"Yeah, that one, Grandma. Well, there's another one of her, but it's not framed—it's in a blue folder in the bookshelf—and she's with some other woman in a fancy dress, standing by a river. Do you remember that one?"

"Yes, yes. That was taken by George Fiske, before Clare was even a park ranger. He was a very famous Yosemite photographer, took all sorts of wonderful pictures in the park."

Lizzie hadn't thought for a second about who might have taken the photograph. She'd been way too interested in who was in it. But Grandma May continued,

"There are other pictures of his on the bookshelf—did you see the one of John Muir's cabin?"

Tyler nudged Lizzie.

"You mean John Muir's lost cabin?" Lizzie asked eagerly.

"Well, it wasn't lost to John Muir," Grandma May corrected her. "He certainly knew where it was."

"Yes, that one—that's what I was calling to ask you about."

"Muir had two cabins in Yosemite, supposedly," Grandma May continued. "Nobody knows exactly where they were."

"But they might still be there, right?" Lizzie asked.

"Oh, I doubt that," Grandma May said dismissively. "They probably rotted away a long time ago. I expect they were just shacks, really . . . not built to last. But I'm so glad you're interested in those photos of Clare Hodges! Your mother was named for her, you know."

"Yes, Grandma, I remember," Lizzie said impatiently. "The thing I wanted to ask was, in the other photo of Clare Hodges, by the stream, it looks like John Muir's cabin is in the background. Do you remember that?"

"No, I can't say that I do," Grandma May said. "I'll have to look at it again when I visit. But it wouldn't surprise me. As I said, George Fiske took the picture of Muir's cabin, and he took that second picture of Clare and Kitty Tatch."

"Is that the other woman in the picture?" Lizzie asked. "Because that's what we—" Tyler jabbed her and Lizzie caught herself. "I mean, that's what I was wondering."

"Kitty Tatch? Oh, she's a legend!" Grandma May exclaimed. "You can still buy postcards of her dancing on top of Overhanging Rock."

Tyler squinted at Lizzie in bewilderment, but she only shrugged. She was used to her grandmother's conversational detours.

"But who is Kitty Tatch?"

"Well," Grandma May began. "She was a waitress at the Sentinel Hotel around 1900, and boy, oh boy, was she something. Everybody in the park knew her name. She and her friend Katherine Hazelston would dress in their ruffled skirts and dancing shoes and go up to Overhanging Rock, at Glacier Point—do you remember Overhanging Rock, Lizzie? I took you there, but it was four or five years ago."

"I don't think so. What is it?"

"Just what the name says. It's a ledge of rock that sticks straight out over the valley, very, very high up."

"Oh, now I remember," Lizzie said. She had a vague recollection of holding her grandmother's hand and standing on top of a huge, flat rock, looking out over the immense depth of the valley.

"Well, it was popular with tourists to have their pictures taken on top of it, because it looked so dangerous. And it *was* so dangerous—if you slipped off, you would tumble thousands of feet to your death. So, anyway, Kitty Tatch went up there with her friend Katherine and they danced and did the can-can—you know, high kicks—with their feet sticking out over the edge. And George Fiske took their photograph."

"He did? Way up on that ledge?"

"Yes, and it was turned into a postcard—a very famous one." Lizzie could hear the smile in Grandma May's voice. "You can still buy it. Kitty Tatch would sell signed copies of them. If you look under my bed, you'll find one. There's a stack of books and I use the postcard as a bookmark."

Lizzie raised her eyebrows at Tyler. "Really?"

"Yes. It's a magnificent picture."

Tyler sprang up and trotted down the hall to the bedroom. He returned with a delighted grin flashing across his face, waving a shiny, brown-tinted postcard. He held it out to Lizzie, who caught her breath. The

photo showed a high bluff in the distance, with a sharp ledge sticking out horizontally over a deep valley. On top of it, very close to the edge, were two tiny female figures in long skirts, each kicking a leg out over the void.

"Wow!" Lizzie exclaimed. "I'm looking at it now."

"Isn't it remarkable?" Grandma May said. "Even in our day! Think how it must have seemed to people at the time. Women led lives that were so limited back then. They couldn't work at most jobs; they weren't allowed to vote. And here were these two common waitresses living in the valley, all dressed up in their finery, dancing on the edge of oblivion."

"It is a great picture," Lizzie said. Now she felt as curious about the photographer who had taken it as she did about the two women dancing on the ledge, thousands of feet up in the air.

"Yosemite at that time," Grandma May continued, "was chock-full of characters. So many free spirits! Including our cousin Clare. It was still the frontier, really, so society's normal rules didn't apply."

Lizzie considered this. It was hard to picture a place where you didn't have to follow the rules. It seemed like every place she had ever been, from the zoo to school to church to the doctor's office, had some set of rules that restricted behavior. A place without rules—what would that be like? She glanced at Tyler and she could tell from his wistful expression that he was thinking exactly the same thing.

"Ask about the cabin," he whispered to her.

She nodded and leaned over the phone. "Clare knew Yosemite really well, didn't she, Grandma? Since she was a park ranger?"

"Oh, yes. She rode all over the place on that horse of hers, even before she was a ranger."

"So she must have known where John Muir's cabin was. I mean, we have a picture of her there. Did she ever mention it to you?"

"Not that I recall," Grandma May answered. "But it wouldn't surprise me if she knew its location. There weren't that many houses or buildings in Yosemite in the early 1900s . . . and obviously, George Fiske knew where it was, since he photographed it."

Lizzie thought for a minute. "I want to go to Yosemite when you come to visit. Could we do that? Camping?"

Tyler tugged her sleeve and pointed at himself. "What about me?" he mouthed.

"I might bring a friend," Lizzie added quickly. "And could we look for John Muir's lost cabin?"

"Oh, honey, I think my camping days are over," Grandma May said with a sigh. "But I would be happy to take you to Yosemite and stay in a hotel in the park.

And then we could explore wherever you want. Though I doubt we'll find anything left of John Muir's cabin."

"That would be great, Grandma." Lizzie smiled into the phone. "I can't wait for you to come."

"I can't wait, either, Lizzie—I miss you way too much! Oh my goodness, it's nearly two o'clock. My bridge group will be waiting. . . . They are all very punctual. Love you, honey. Bye!"

"Love you too, Grandma," Lizzie answered. "Bye." She hung up the phone.

Tyler was watching her, his expression puzzled.

"What?"

"You and her sound . . . tight," he said finally.

"We are," Lizzie replied. "She's my grandma."

"I know, but it's not like she lives here. How often do you even see her?"

"Well, she used to live here when I was little. Now she's in a retirement place in Arizona, but she still comes to visit every few months. And I talk to her a lot." Lizzie slid the phone into the kitchen wall-mount and turned back to him. Something in his face made her feel like she should apologize. "Maybe it's because of my mom," she said. "I'm all my grandma has left of her, you know?"

Tyler didn't say anything.

Lizzie joined him again on the couch, resting her feet on the coffee table next to his. "What's the matter?" she asked.

When he didn't answer, she said, "Do you miss your mom?"

He still didn't answer, so she tried again. "I miss my mom sometimes."

At that, his dark eyes flashed at her. "What are you talking about? You never even knew your mom."

She recoiled, stung by his words. Then suddenly she felt mad. "Well, your mom is still alive, right? And you're here. So if you're missing your mom, it's your own fault."

Tyler's hands balled into fists. "That's a lie," he snapped. "None of it was my fault. And what do you know, anyway? You think you've got it so rough, cuz your mom died when you were born. My mom's still alive but it's like she's not even there. It's worse than her being dead."

"What are you talking about? What's the big secret about your mom?" Lizzie demanded. "I told you how my mom died. And you even said it was my fault! Which it wasn't. But your mom is still alive. How can you say that's worse?"

Tyler was sitting opposite her with his face crunched in a furious glower. It reminded her of how he'd looked when she'd first confronted him about the stolen food tray . . . which was only a couple of days ago, she realized with a start.

"I'll tell you how it's worse. Cuz your mom *can't* be with you. If she was here, you know she'd . . ." He lapsed into silence.

"What?" Lizzie asked.

"She'd take care of you." He looked away suddenly. "My mom could do that, but she won't."

He was breathing heavily now, and Lizzie saw him blink hard, twice. She felt suddenly cowed, afraid he was going to cry.

"Okay," she said. "We don't have to talk about it."

Tyler jumped up and went over to the kitchen, his back to her. "I'm just saying," he mumbled, his voice steadier, "that mine is worse." He took a glass from the cabinet and filled it with water at the sink, guzzling it down.

Lizzie watched him, overcome by an almost unbearable sadness. She didn't know anything about her mother, really. Clare was a shimmering mirage, a person she had never even met. But the thing she was sure of, had always been sure of for as long as she could remember, was that her mother had wanted her and loved her, from the very first beat of her heart. Was it because her father had always told her that? And her grandmother, too? Lizzie wasn't sure, but she realized, for as many things as she didn't know about her own mother, the things Tyler *did* know about his mother were much, much worse. She thought of the photograph in his backpack, the smiling teenager with the long blond hair. What could she have done that was so terrible? Why wasn't she here, taking care of Tyler?

Tyler set the empty glass down on the counter with a clack. "Let's get out of here," he said. "We can check on the wolves."

"Sure," Lizzie agreed, feeling exhausted herself. She gathered the old photographs together and settled them back in the blue folder. "This one is pretty cool, though, right?" she said, lifting the postcard.

"Yeah, it is," Tyler agreed. "Crazy."

"And Grandma May will take us to Yosemite! To look for the lost cabin."

"Yeah. Maybe."

Lizzie knew they were both wondering how that could ever happen. How would she explain him to Grandma May?

She touched his shoulder. "We'll figure something out," she said.

Together, they thudded down the stairs to the door. Lizzie pushed it open, and they walked out into the afternoon sunlight.

And there, coming down the driveway, was Mike.

RUNAWAY

THEY FROZE IN their tracks as Mike walked toward them, a questioning look on his face. Lizzie could sense Tyler's fear. She knew he was ready to bolt. "Stay put," she whispered.

"Hey," she called, trying to sound as normal as possible. "What are you doing here?" Her father almost never came home in the middle of the work day.

"Hi," he said. "Were you in the apartment?"

She nodded. "This is my friend Tyler. I was showing him those old pictures of Yosemite."

Mike came to stand in front of them, still looking puzzled. "Hi, Tyler," he said.

"Hey," Tyler mumbled, looking at the pavement.

Mike turned to Lizzie. "A friend from school?"

"We ran into each other in the zoo," she said. That part was true at least.

"Oh." He paused, looking at Lizzie, and she could see from his face that something was wrong.

"What's the matter? Why are you home so early?"

"I'm not. I have to go back. I just came to tell you . . ." He glanced at Tyler. "Karen called. Tamarack died."

"What?" Lizzie gasped, biting her lip. She could feel her eyes filling. "But we just took her to the clinic a couple of hours ago! How could she have died already? I thought you were calling another vet."

Mike wrapped his arms around her, hugging her close. "We were, honey. But she had a fever, and I don't know . . . maybe the move traumatized her."

"You said she was going to be okay."

"I thought so. I was wrong. And Lizzie . . ."

She buried her face into his rough coveralls, breathing the dense, musky animal smells. His arms tightened over her shoulders. "Lobo is throwing up."

She pushed back from him, staring.

"I wanted to tell you myself."

"No." She could barely speak.

"Karen and Ed isolated him, and she's talking to a vet up in Seattle. We're trying to figure it out."

"But he was fine this morning! You saw him!" Her heart was pounding, the sound filling her ears. *Not Lobo.*

"Lizzie, whatever it is, it comes on quickly. Karen, Ed, and I need to move him to the clinic. Then I have to go back to check on the other wolves."

She stood still, not looking at him. She could feel her father and Tyler staring at her.

"Honey," Mike said, "we're doing everything we can for them." He rested his hand on her head, and the heavy warmth of it anchored her. "You stay here. I just came home to tell you."

She nodded mutely, her throat aching. All she could think of was Lobo, watching her with his pale silver eyes. The whole summer, whenever she sat close to Wolf Woods looking at him, she'd felt connected to something deep and mysterious and *wild.* She couldn't bear to think that he might die.

"I probably won't be back till late," Mike said, "but you can get something to eat at the snack bar. You too, Tyler, if you want to stay for dinner."

He squeezed her shoulder, glanced again at Tyler, then turned and walked away.

As soon as he had disappeared around the curve of the driveway, Tyler turned to Lizzie, his face panicked. "I have to go."

Still overwhelmed with the news about Lobo, she could only stare at him blankly. "Why?"

"Because he knows I'm here!" Tyler cried.

"What's wrong with that? I've had friends over before. He doesn't know you're staying in the apartment."

Tyler was pacing back and forth, running his hands over his springy crop of black curls. "This is how it starts. He'll ask questions. He'll figure it out."

Lizzie took a deep breath. "Tyler, calm down. He's too worried about the wolves right now to think about anything else. I am, too. And you should be," she added reproachfully.

Tyler collapsed in the grass at the edge of the driveway, covering his face with his hands. "I knew it was too good to be true. I knew it."

"You're freaking out for no reason," Lizzie protested.

Tyler shook his head, breathing hard. "You don't know what it's like."

Lizzie squatted next to him and looked straight into his anxious eyes. "No, I don't. But Tyler, listen. We won't let anything bad happen. We won't."

"It won't be up to us." He jumped to his feet and ran across the yard toward the apartment.

"What are you doing?" Lizzie chased after him.

"Packing my stuff."

"That's crazy. My dad doesn't know anything about you. He's not going to turn you in."

Tyler tugged the side door of the garage till it squeaked open, then pounded up the narrow steps to the apartment. Lizzie ran after him.

"But you just got here," she pleaded. "Don't you want to stay?"

He whipped around. "Yeah, of course I do! I never had a place like this in my whole entire life. But I can't now. I have to get out of here."

He snatched his backpack from the floor and began stuffing his now-clean clothing into it.

Lizzie grabbed his arm. "Tyler, stop. Can you just slow down for a minute? If you really want to leave—" At the look on his face, she amended, "If you really think you have to leave, I'll help you. But my dad won't be back until late. You heard him. So let's just hang out for a while. We'll make sure you have everything and then we'll go to the snack bar, like my dad said, and get something to eat. You should take food with you, right?

And there's a bus back into town that comes by the zoo gate at closing."

Tyler sat on his heels, his half-filled backpack cradled in his lap. "I don't have money for the bus," he said.

"I have a bus pass," Lizzie said promptly. "I'll give it to you. Then you can go anywhere you want."

He was still breathing hard, but he seemed to hesitate.

"Aren't you hungry?" she asked, more gently. "We can have something to eat here, that stuff we brought over yesterday. Then you can pack up."

He slid the backpack off his lap. "Okay," he said resignedly. "But then I'm leaving."

He looked around the quiet apartment, and Lizzie watched his gaze move from the tidy kitchen to the sunny living room and to the open doorway of the bedroom. The expression on his face suddenly seemed like the saddest thing she had ever seen. Where would he go?

Chapter 16

AT THE CLINIC

THEY SPENT THE afternoon in the sunny apartment, snacking on potato chips, apples, and peanut butter, and organizing Tyler's few possessions. Lizzie got her journal from her bedroom and curled up on the blue sofa to write about the wolves. She couldn't stop thinking about Lobo.

"What is that thing?" Tyler asked. "You carry it everywhere."

She looked at him in surprise. "Didn't I tell you? It's my notebook. My summer homework."

"Summer homework?" He recoiled. "That's crazy."

She smiled at him. "I know. But it's not graded.

We're supposed to keep a nature journal, like John Muir did."

"So what kind of stuff are you writing?"

"Oh, just things about trees and flowers and the animals at the zoo. Mostly about the wolves."

"Read me something."

Lizzie frowned. "I don't read it to anyone. It's just for me." At his disappointed look, she said, "Here, I can read you something John Muir wrote. I copied a bunch of his quotes." She flipped to the front of the notebook and found one she liked. *"Everybody needs beauty as well as bread, places to play in and pray in, where Nature may heal and cheer and give strength to body and soul alike."*

What would John Muir say about the wolves? she wondered. He seemed to believe so passionately in the goodness of nature, that nature made no mistakes. But the wolves were dying.

"Huh," Tyler said thoughtfully. "He sounds kind of religious."

Lizzie nodded. "He was religious about nature."

"I think people need bread more than beauty." Tyler stood at the kitchen counter, studying the supply of food. "I know I do." He put two apples and two bottles of water in the backpack, then drummed his fingers on

the countertop fretfully. "We're going to get more food at the snack bar, right? Before I leave?"

"Sure," Lizzie said. "As much as you can carry."

An hour later, they sat in a corner of the food court at a table heaped with food. The zoo was closing now, so the other tables were empty, with throngs of people walking through the plaza toward the exit gates. Lizzie knew that this was basically a last meal. Even though they weren't hungry after snacking all afternoon, Tyler had ordered almost everything on the menu. Behind the counter, Sonya had laughingly piled their selections on two trays, asking, "Are you having a party? This can't be for just the two of you!" And now the bounty was spread before them: two hot dogs, two hamburgers, a cheese pizza, onion rings *and* french fries, two chocolate chip cookies, and two jumbo lemonades. Lizzie barely felt like eating; she was too worried about Lobo, and now worried about where Tyler would go next. But Tyler suffered no such inhibition. He steadily worked his way through the feast, while Lizzie drew a picture of Lobo in her notebook. From the summer of watching him, she knew his face by heart.

"Hey, that's pretty good," Tyler said, stuffing an onion ring into his mouth and crunching loudly.

Lizzie held it away from her, studying it critically. "Not really. I like to draw, but I'm not good at it."

"Well, I can tell it's Lobo," Tyler said.

Lizzie looked at him in surprise. "Really? How?"

"Cuz he has that stripe of darker fur in the middle of his head." He gestured with one greasy finger. At her expression, he snorted. "You think you're the only one who can tell them apart? I bet I've spent more time looking at them than you have."

"No way," Lizzie said. "I've been writing about them all summer." She waved the notebook in his face. "But," she said begrudgingly, "it's good that you can tell it's Lobo. I guess I'm a pretty good drawer after all."

"Or I'm good at—" Tyler shrugged. "Animals."

Lizzie started to argue the point, but then decided it was true. "Yeah, you are," she said.

They looked at each other over the mound of half-eaten food. "I wish you didn't have to go," she added.

She was going to miss him, she realized suddenly. Not even her best friends, Margaret included, paid as much attention to the animals as she did.

"Believe me, me too," Tyler said, shaking his head.

"Your grandma's place was a sweet setup." He sighed. "But it's time for me to leave."

"Where will you go?" Lizzie thought of town. Sometimes she saw homeless people lying on the sidewalk near the grocery store parking lot, wearing too many clothes. She flinched. "By the grocery store?"

"Nah, that place is nasty."

"Are you sure you can't go back home? I mean, to your foster family?"

Tyler's face clouded. "Nobody there that I want to see right now."

Lizzie started to ask about Jesse, but she could tell he wasn't in the mood to discuss it. She tried a different approach. "Aren't you getting tired of sleeping on the ground?"

He shrugged. "I like being outside. Without everybody in my face, you know? On my own."

Stung, Lizzie fell silent. Did he mean that he liked that better than being with her?

Tyler shoved her gently. "Hey. I didn't mean *you*." When she couldn't help smiling, he added, "You're in my face but that's just how you are. Like those goats in the Barnyard."

"*What?*" Lizzie protested. He laughed and gathered the ample remains of their dinner order.

"You should have some," he said. "Whatever you don't eat, I'm taking with me."

Lizzie shook her head. "I don't feel like eating. I want to check on Lobo."

"Me too. But Lobo's not at Wolf Woods anymore, right?"

"No. My dad said they were taking him to the clinic."

He took a long swig of lemonade. "Okay, help me wrap this stuff up."

Lizzie got a plastic bag from Sonya and added some napkins; then they carefully packed everything on top of the clothing in Tyler's backpack. When Tyler zipped it shut, it was bulging and smelled of cheese, onions, and fried food. He heaved it over his shoulder.

"Let's go."

It was almost dark when they reached the clinic, but two outdoor floodlights cast an arc of white light over the yard. Lizzie saw the large pickup truck, its bed empty now. She felt a tense jolt of worry course through her. How could Lobo be sick? He was by far the biggest and strongest of the pack. She tried to shake off her fear. He had to be all right.

She and Tyler stood close to the fence, near a dense hedge of oleander. The pale blossoms glowed a ghostly pink in the dusk.

"This is where I usually watch from," Tyler told her. "Cuz you're shielded by the bushes. And you can see through that window."

Lizzie was struck again by the secret world he'd been privy to, hiding out at the zoo and roaming around at night, when the crowds were gone. Maybe he really did know more about the animals than she did. Even during the day, Tyler had figured out how to make himself disappear; it seemed a valuable trick, when Lizzie thought about it, a kind of freedom.

All while she'd been studying the wolves and writing in her journal, she'd wished she could do so without them being aware of her. She wanted to see their truest, wildest selves, and they were never totally relaxed with people watching them. She'd read once that you could never know exactly what your own face looked like, because the expression you wore when you looked at yourself in the mirror wasn't the expression you wore in real life. It seemed the same with the wolves . . . when someone was watching, they never acted the way they really were.

Sighing, Lizzie craned to see through the clinic

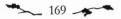

window. The office was empty. She knew the examination and treatment rooms were on the other side of the building. From this vantage point, it was impossible to tell what was going on back there.

"Where is everybody?" Tyler demanded. "The truck's here. The lights are on."

"Sick animals are taken to the back," Lizzie told him.

"Can we walk around to that side and look in?"

Lizzie shook her head. "It's fenced off."

Tyler frowned. "Can we get in through that gate over there?" He gestured to the gate at the corner of the clinic yard.

"No, you need a code," Lizzie said. "And Karen would never let us in. My dad wouldn't, either. Not with Lobo in there."

"Then let's climb the fence," Tyler suggested.

Lizzie scanned the barrier of chain link. It was at least eight feet high. "How? It's too tall."

"No, it's not," Tyler scoffed. "I could climb this in my sleep. Come on, I'll help you."

"If you can do it, I can," Lizzie answered, annoyed. "But what if someone sees us?"

"Don't you want to check on the wolves? Follow me." Tyler dropped his backpack on the ground and ducked into the leafy screen of oleander.

Filled with trepidation, Lizzie put her notebook on top of the backpack and pushed her way through the bushes. Her shoulder scraped against the metal fence. A few feet ahead, Tyler was already scaling the chain link, shoving the toes of his sneakers into the mesh and gripping the diamond-shaped openings high above to haul himself up. One sneaker slipped out, squeaking on the metal, and Tyler's whole body clanged against the fence.

"Watch out," Lizzie whispered. "Somebody will hear you."

"Relax, I just slipped. I've got it now." Grunting, he heaved himself up to the top of the fence, then lifted one leg over. "Look at me!" he called softly down to her. "I'm king of the zoo."

"How are you going to get down?" Lizzie asked, but the words were no sooner out of her mouth than he swung himself over, gripped the top mesh briefly, and then dropped several feet straight to the ground. He landed with a thud and stumbled backward, regaining his balance. "See? Easy. Now you."

So much for the help, Lizzie thought. She scrutinized the fence doubtfully. It occurred to her that he'd had practice at this.

"Okay, here goes," she said. Wedging the toe of her sneaker into the mesh about two feet from the ground, she reached up with both hands as far as possible to grasp the chain link. She pulled herself up and clung to the sheet of fencing like a monkey.

"Good!" Tyler encouraged her. "Keep going."

Lizzie had never felt so precarious in her life. The metal was biting into the tip of her sneaker, which seemed ready to slip from its tenuous purchase at any moment. She reached her hands up to grip a higher section of fence, and then, balancing on her more secure foot, took another step up, hauling herself higher. The cold metal pinched her fingers. Just as she was about to pull herself up to the top, she heard something.

"Shhhhh!" Tyler warned, whipping around toward the clinic. Lizzie, clinging to the fence with all her might, saw that the empty front office was no longer empty. On the other side of the big rectangular window, her father and Karen had appeared. Her father was heading toward the door.

"Tyler, hide!" she whispered frantically. "They're coming out."

Tyler raced across the dusty yard to the truck and dove underneath it, rolling out of sight. Lizzie could see her father reaching for the door handle. In desperation, she released her hold on the chain link and tumbled back into the bushes, scrambling to the ground.

The door of the clinic swung open. Lizzie crouched under the shield of oleander branches, holding her breath. She scanned the area around the truck to make sure there was no sign of Tyler. Then, just as her father stepped onto the porch, she saw Tyler's backpack, out in the open on her side of the fence, with her green notebook lying on top. Quickly, she grabbed the strap and, with a soft swish, yanked it under the bushes.

"I just can't believe it," Mike was saying. Lizzie could hear the tension in his voice. "I don't think I've ever seen an animal go downhill so quickly."

Was it Lobo? Lizzie's pulse raced. She leaned closer to the fence so she could hear.

"I don't think he'll make it through the night," Karen answered soberly.

"We need an autopsy."

"Yes." Karen followed him into the yard. "I'll take care of it."

"On Tamarack, too. We should have done it for Athena."

Lizzie could see their faces clearly now, her father's creased with worry.

"I know. I'm sorry." Karen touched his arm, and Lizzie started, remembering their other relationship, the one that had nothing to do with the zoo.

He shook his head. "I'm not blaming you," he said quickly. "I know they're your top priority. But to protect the rest of the pack . . . and, well, the board will ask me."

"I'll take care of it," Karen said again. "If Lobo dies, I have someone in Fresno who can do it. I'll go tonight."

"No, I didn't mean that," Mike said. "I can ride with you tomorrow. I hope we won't have to. I hope it turns around. He's a big guy, stronger than the others."

"Yes," Karen said. "But the fever and the tremors . . ." She stopped. "We need to know what this is as soon as possible."

Mike nodded. "Call me if anything happens, and we'll figure it out. I'm going to head over and check on the other four."

He squeezed Karen's shoulder, much the way he would squeeze Lizzie's when he wanted to reassure her. Then he walked toward the gate.

Lizzie could barely breathe.

Chapter 17

STRANGE TREATMENT

AS SOON AS her father had left the clinic yard and Karen had reentered the building, Lizzie stood up and brushed herself off.

"Tyler," she whispered, her eyes glued to the quiet area where the truck sat. After a minute, she saw his legs wriggling under the bumper, and he pushed himself out into the open.

"Whoa, that was close," he said softly, running toward her. "Give me my backpack! I forgot about it."

"Yeah, I know," Lizzie complained. "You left it where anybody could see it."

Tyler shrugged. "Good thing you grabbed it."

"Yeah, good thing." She picked up one strap of the backpack. "Should I throw it over?"

"Sure. But careful! There's a lot of food in there. I don't want it banging around."

"I'm putting my notebook inside. Don't forget to give it back to me."

Lizzie stuffed her notebook into the backpack and glanced nervously at the window of the clinic. The front room was empty again. Karen must have returned to the sick wolf. She pushed her way out of the bushes, holding Tyler's backpack aloft.

"It's heavy," she said, positioning herself a few feet from the fence. "Okay, here goes."

She began to swing it. The first time she let go, the backpack sailed up through the air, hit the top of the fence, and promptly tumbled back toward the ground.

"Catch it!" Tyler cried.

"Shhhh," Lizzie warned, rushing forward with arms outstretched. The heavy backpack hit them with a thud, and Lizzie almost fell over.

"You have to do better than that," Tyler protested. "I don't want the food to spill all over my clothes."

Lizzie glared at him. She grabbed the strap and began to swing the backpack again, more forcefully.

When she released it this time, it lofted over the fence, and Tyler ran to catch it.

"Good one," he said happily. "Now climb over so we can see what's going on with Lobo."

Easier said than done, Lizzie thought. She shouldered through the bushes and began to pull herself up the chain link of the fence—foot, hand, hand, foot, hand, hand—heaving herself higher.

"You got it," Tyler urged, his voice low. "Keep going."

"What do I do now?" Lizzie asked, clinging to the wobbly top of the fence. The ground on the other side seemed a long way down.

"You have to swing your leg over," Tyler told her. "The way I did."

One thing Lizzie felt sure of: She was not going to be able to swing her leg over the way Tyler did.

"I don't think—"

"Try."

It took all of Lizzie's strength to pull her torso over the rough top of the fence and heave one leg over. Now she was straddling the chain link uncomfortably, clinging to the metal wire, feeling the edges dig into her flesh.

"That's it!" Tyler urged. "Jam your foot into the fence and swing your other leg over."

Lizzie tried to do as he said, wedging the toe of her sneaker into the mesh, but just as she was climbing over the bar at the top, her foot slipped and she started to fall. Tyler dove beneath her so that her sneaker landed on his back.

"Whoa!" Lizzie cried.

"You're okay. Stand on me."

With one foot teetering back and forth on Tyler's backbone, she adjusted her grip on the fence and lowered her other leg to a new purchase.

"Okay, okay," she told him breathlessly. "Now I'm good."

Finally, she dropped to the ground.

"See? That was great!" Tyler said.

Lizzie took a shuddering breath and glanced at the shadowy contours of the clinic. The building was quiet now.

"C'mon." Tyler lifted his backpack to his shoulder. "Where's Lobo?"

"Follow me." Lizzie walked quietly under the big window, which shone bright and empty, and peered around the edge of the building.

"There, in the back corner," she told Tyler. "That's the treatment room."

Its window was also brightly lit.

"Be really quiet," Lizzie whispered, "so we can get close enough to see what's going on."

They tiptoed along the back of the concrete building until they neared the window. Lizzie had only been in the treatment room once before. A year ago, a baby impala had broken its leg and she'd been with her father when he carried the little antelope to the vet. The room was large and antiseptic-looking, with a white tile floor and tall metal cabinets along one wall. There were two broad stainless steel examination tables in the center. On one of these rested a large transport cage, with a wolf inside.

When Lizzie saw Lobo, she gasped. The massive wolf was lying on his side, his limbs jerking. Her eyes filled with tears.

"Oh! Look at him," she whispered.

Tyler stood beside her, frozen.

"He's dying." She could barely speak. Her throat burned. She thought of the long, hot days in June and July when she had sat mere feet away from him, breathing his smell, watching him flick his ears or sniff the air or trot purposefully across the enclosure toward the rest of the pack.

Fierce, massive Lobo, with his burning silver eyes . . . he was so strong and sure and smart. It seemed impossible that he'd been reduced to this fragile state.

 179

Tyler turned to her. "Is that Tamarack?" he asked, pointing.

Lizzie saw that in a corner of the room was another cage, with a blanket partially covering it. A mound of light fur filled it, lifeless.

Lizzie covered her mouth with her hand.

Suddenly, Tyler grabbed her arm and pulled her close to the wall of the building. "Shhhh. Somebody's coming."

Together they peered over the windowsill. Lizzie heard the faint sound of footsteps, and then saw the door in the corner of the room swing open. Karen, her blond ponytail bobbing, strode quickly toward the cages.

Lizzie stood on her toes to see better. Karen had a capped syringe in her hand. She set it on the edge of the steel examination table where Lobo lay in his cage. Then she pulled on blue surgical gloves, snapping them in place. She seemed to be talking to Lobo, murmuring in a low monotone, but Lizzie couldn't hear what she was saying. Karen was so much better with animals than with people, Lizzie thought, not for the first time. It was hard to have a conversation with her—she could be so cold and blunt—but with a sick animal, she was unfailingly patient and gentle.

"What's she doing?" Tyler whispered.

Lizzie shook her head. "Giving him medicine, I guess."

Karen uncapped the syringe and lifted it in the air, pressing the plunger to ready it for injection. With her free hand, she unlatched the door of the cage.

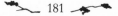

Lizzie stiffened. "She's not supposed to do that. You never open the cages without somebody else to help."

"Maybe she thinks he's too sick to hurt her?" Tyler whispered.

Lobo jerked and heaved, but he was too weak to get away from her. They watched as Karen, with one swift motion, held his massive head against the cage floor and stabbed the needle into his shoulder. Then she closed the cage door and latched it. Within minutes, Lobo's legs stopped spasming. He lay still.

Lizzie's heart clutched. "What did she do? You don't think she—" She turned to Tyler in horror.

He was pressed close to the window, furiously biting his lip.

"Did she put the other one to sleep?" he asked Lizzie. "Is that what your dad said?"

Lizzie shook her head. "No, Tamarack died, remember? But she put Athena to sleep." Her whole body was trembling now, unable to believe what they'd witnessed.

"Maybe she just gave him something to make his legs stop jerking around like that," Tyler said doubtfully.

"But look." Lizzie could barely speak. "He's not moving at all. I can't even see him breathing."

Tyler's eyes were riveted on Lobo. "Why would she do that?"

Lizzie crowded closer and watched as Karen ripped off the gloves and threw them in the metal trash receptacle along with the syringe. She picked up the phone on the clinic wall. Through the glass they could hear her muted voice.

"Hi, Ed, it's Karen. There's no need for you to come in tonight: They're both gone." There was a pause, and then she said more hurriedly, "Yeah, Lobo, too. Still no idea what it is. Mike is over checking on the others. I'll call you later."

What had she done? Lizzie couldn't stand it. She wanted to break through the glass and stop whatever was happening.

But in her heart she knew it was too late. She stared at Lobo's huge, inert body inside the cage.

No! she screamed inside her head. She pressed against the window, fully exposed now. *No.*

"Lobo," Tyler whispered.

Karen started to leave the room. Suddenly, she whipped around.

Tyler grabbed Lizzie's arm and they both dropped to the ground on all fours. Lizzie was sure Karen had seen them, but when she peered over the windowsill again,

183

Karen strode back to the trash can and opened it, pulling the drawstring on the garbage bag and taking it with her. She left the room, propping the door open on her way out.

In their cages, the two wolves lay silent and still.

Lizzie and Tyler stared at each other, and Lizzie could feel the tears spilling down her cheeks.

Lobo was dead.

STOWAWAYS

TYLER SHOOK HER shoulder, his face fierce. "She killed him."

Lizzie could only stare in disbelief at the lifeless bodies of the wolves. Tears burned her eyes.

"Why do you think she did that? Why not just let him die?" he persisted.

When she didn't answer, Tyler nodded, more to himself than to Lizzie. "It's okay. Maybe she was trying to put him out of his pain. That's what vets do, right?"

That was, of course, what vets did. Her father believed it was the one thing vets *could* do that human doctors didn't do often enough . . . stop a creature from suffering when the end was near and there was no hope of recovery.

But everything about this seemed wrong.

"Lizzie?"

Lizzie turned to him.

"It's pretty late now," he said quietly. "You should probably go back home, you know?"

She nodded, full of despair. "What about you? Where will you go?"

"I'll be okay. I'll stay around here tonight and then find someplace new tomorrow."

"Will I see you again?"

"Sure," Tyler said. "I'll come back to the zoo to visit."

"Really? I have some money," she said hurriedly. "My dad makes me carry it for emergencies." She fished in her pocket. "Here, take this." She handed him a ten-dollar bill.

Tyler hesitated. "For real? You don't need it?"

She shook her head. "This is my emergency."

He smiled a little. "Okay. Thanks."

"And you have my bus pass, right? So you can come back?"

He nodded. Lizzie squared her shoulders, trying to be strong. She cast one long glance back at the still

bodies of the wolves, then led the way around the building to the front yard. She wouldn't think about Lobo
now. She couldn't bear to.

"Do we have to climb the fence again?" Tyler asked.

Lizzie shook her head. "We can go out through the
access gate. From the inside, you just have to press a
button. But it makes a lot of noise. I guess we should
wait till Karen leaves."

Tyler shifted from one foot to the other. "How long
will that take?"

"I don't know, but—" Lizzie was about to say,
"there's nothing left for her to do," but then they heard
the loud metallic rumble of the garage door going up
and bright light spread across the darkening yard.

"Hide!" Lizzie barely had time to whisper. She and
Tyler crouched at the corner of the building, just as
Karen hurried out of the garage and hopped into the
truck.

Was she leaving?

The engine roared to life, but instead of driving out
of the clinic yard, Karen reversed the truck into the
open garage.

"What's she doing?" Tyler whispered.

"I don't know," Lizzie answered in confusion.

They leaned around the corner of the building to

peer into the bright box of the garage. Karen had shut off the engine and now she was lowering the truck's tailgate so that the empty bed of the truck butted against the clinic's loading dock. Then she ran up the steps into the building.

Lizzie turned to Tyler. "She's going to load something into the truck. This way she can roll it straight from floor level onto the tailgate."

They waited. They could hear Karen clanging around inside, exclaiming softly as she struggled with something. Then she appeared at the loading dock with a trolley and balanced across it was the cage with Tamarack's white body inside.

"The wolves!" Tyler hissed. "She's taking their bodies somewhere."

They watched as Karen maneuvered the cage onto the open tailgate and then shoved it toward the back of the truck bed, the metal scraping loudly. Barely pausing, she grabbed the handle of the trolley and strode quickly down the hall. As soon as she was gone, Tyler crept around the corner of the building, into the garage.

"Tyler! What are you doing?" Lizzie whispered. "She'll see you."

"No, she won't," he called softly. "I'll stay out of sight. I just want to see what's going on."

Nervously, Lizzie followed him. They could hear Karen in the back of the building, grunting and moving something.

Together, they leaned over the side of the truck bed. It was empty except for the cage with Tamarack, shoved against the cab, and an old wool blanket wadded up against the side.

They heard wheels rattling down the hallway, and Tyler immediately bolted for the open garage door. Lizzie followed him, ducking out of the line of sight.

"Where would she be taking them?" Tyler whispered.

Lizzie shook her head. "I don't know. Maybe to Fresno, for the autopsy? But she was supposed to call my dad. He wanted to go with her."

"She seems like she's in a hurry," Tyler said.

"Look," Lizzie whispered. "She's got Lobo now." She couldn't suppress a gasp at the sight of his big body heaped on the floor of the cage. He looked smaller to her somehow. Poor Lobo. She swallowed a sob.

They watched as Karen struggled with the second cage, bumping it from the trolley onto the tailgate and again shoving it toward the cab of the truck, while the wolf's body bounced lifelessly against the frame.

Tyler frowned. "Remember how I told you I saw a

truck with a cage leaving the clinic the other night? It was like this."

"That doesn't make sense," Lizzie said, her eyes riveted on Karen.

In a series of quick motions, Karen shut off the lights inside the clinic, pulled down the rolling door of the loading dock, and slammed the truck's tailgate closed.

"She's ready to go," Tyler said urgently. "Come on."

Lizzie stared at him. "What do you mean?"

"Don't you want to see where she's taking them?"

"Yes, but we can't—"

Just then, the engine roared and the truck emerged from the garage, rolling across the yard toward the access gate. The garage door jolted down behind it.

Before Lizzie could even understand what was happening, Tyler hoisted his backpack on his shoulder and sped through the dusk to the truck bed, crossing the yard in a few swift bounds. Karen's pale arm reached through the truck window to punch the button that opened the access gate. As the gate creaked loudly, Lizzie watched Tyler heave himself into the dark truck bed from the passenger side. He leaned toward her, beckoning.

Lizzie didn't know what to do. In a minute, the truck, the wolves, and Tyler would be gone.

As the access gate shuddered and ground to a halt, she ran. She reached the passenger side of the truck bed just as the truck started to move. She thought for a minute that she was too late, as the tires crunched loudly over the gravel. But then Tyler strained toward her, and she grabbed his outstretched hand. With her other hand, she gripped the cold metal side of the truck and half tumbled, half slid into the truck bed.

Breathless, she pressed her body flat against its ridged surface in case Karen glanced in the rearview mirror. She huddled there with Tyler and the dead wolves as the truck rumbled out of the zoo and into the night.

Chapter 19

NIGHT RIDE

THE EVENING AIR was cool and sharp, blasting over them as the truck sped up. There had been a few abrupt turns leaving the zoo, but Lizzie could tell that now they were on a highway. She and Tyler lay crammed together in the metal bed, with his backpack wedged between them. Tyler had snatched the wool blanket and spread it over them, whether for warmth or to hide them from Karen's view, Lizzie wasn't sure. The wool scratched against Lizzie's skin and she smelled the warm, musky scent of animals. When she twisted her head, she could see the front of the cages and inside them, the blurry humps of the wolves' bodies. It was dark now.

Lobo! For a minute, his wild, beautiful face loomed before her, the mane of fur, the steady, secret gaze of his silver eyes. Again, she stifled a sob. Even if Karen had done it to save him from pain, there was something so deliberate about taking his life. Her father would call it mercy, the kindness of sparing an animal needless suffering. But at what point did mercy become murder? How could anyone know, really know for certain, that the only future outcome was death?

She felt Tyler turn toward her and she hoped he couldn't see her tears. "You okay?" he asked, close to her cheek.

Lizzie nodded. "What are we going to do when the truck stops? She'll see us."

"We have to jump out before she opens the back."

"But how will we have time?"

"That's what we have to do," Tyler insisted. "At least it's dark, and she's not expecting us to be here."

They rode in silence, staring at the vast sky overhead as it turned inky, with glittering pinpricks of stars. Lizzie could feel every dip and bump in the highway flying past underneath them.

"I can't believe I don't have my cell phone," she said. She pictured the cell phone where she'd left it, on the nightstand in her bedroom.

"Why didn't you bring it? We could sure use it."

"I didn't know I was leaving the zoo," Lizzie countered. "I wasn't planning on a camping trip!"

Even in the dark, she could see Tyler grimace. "I wasn't either! But sometimes stuff happens and you have to change your plans."

Lizzie was thinking that *he* had changed *her* plans by jumping into the truck. But it seemed pointless to argue.

"I'm going to try to see where we're going," Lizzie said against Tyler's ear. The roar of the wind and the rattling of the truck made it hard to hear each other.

"No!" he warned. "If you lift your head and she looks in the mirror, she might see you."

"I'll be careful," Lizzie said. "She could be driving for hours. What if she's going to Mexico?"

The thought had just occurred to her, and as nonsensical as it seemed, she felt a prickle of fear. What would they do if they ended up lost in another country?

"What are you talking about?" Tyler demanded. "Why would she do that?"

"I don't know. But nothing she's doing makes sense. I'm going to take a look."

"You be quick, then," Tyler said.

Carefully, Lizzie rolled onto her stomach. Through the wire bars of the cages and the back window of the truck, she could barely make out the silhouette of Karen's head.

She pressed her palms against the ridged metal bed and pushed up just a few inches. A sudden blaze of oncoming headlights lit the truck, and Tyler yanked her down.

"Watch out!" he whispered.

"Okay, okay." Lizzie waited a minute, then gently raised herself again. The wind stung her face. She could see the highway stretching ahead, straight and empty, with black, looming woods on either side. There were no houses or gas stations or other markers of civilization.

"I think we're going toward the mountains," she told Tyler, holding herself up on her elbows.

"Get down," Tyler cautioned, but Lizzie craned into the darkness. After a few minutes, she glimpsed something in the distance on the edge of the road: a green-and-white highway sign. As the truck hurtled past, it loomed suddenly: *MIDPINES 4*.

Lizzie gasped.

"What?" Tyler demanded, and she dropped back to her stomach so she could tell him.

"We're on the highway to Yosemite."

"Yosemite!" Tyler stared at her. "How do you know?"

"Because we're almost to Midpines. This is the way you get into the park."

"Wow," Tyler breathed, and then, almost to himself, "I'm going to Yosemite."

Lizzie flinched. With all that had happened, how could he be thinking about visiting Yosemite, as if it were a stop on a bus tour? "In the dark, you won't be able to see much," she snapped.

He recoiled slightly, and she instantly felt sorry for how mean she'd sounded. She huddled closer to be heard over the whoosh of wind. "Why would Karen be going to Yosemite?"

Tyler hesitated. "Maybe that's where she's going to dump the bodies."

Lizzie shivered. "But why?"

"I don't know. It's all crazy if you ask me."

They crowded under the blanket, contemplating this, as the truck rumbled down the highway. Its speed had slowed, navigating turns, and Lizzie could feel the air changing, becoming sharper and colder. Her ears popped.

"We're climbing," she told Tyler.

The passing headlights were few and far between now, until there was only darkness. Lizzie thought she heard the rush and gurgle of water. She remembered that there was a stream alongside the road for much of the ride into Yosemite. Was that what she heard now, the sound of water over rocks?

"How long have we been driving?" Tyler asked, and

Lizzie wished she'd thought to check her watch when they left the zoo.

She shrugged against him. "I don't know."

They lay in silence for a while, feeling the truck's vibration beneath them, and then Tyler asked, "Do you hear that?"

"Yeah," Lizzie said. "It's the river. I think we're almost to Yosemite."

"No," Tyler said, his voice hushed. "It's inside the truck."

And then Lizzie heard it, too . . . the muted clang of metal, almost lost in the rush of wind and road noise.

She froze. "Did you bump the cage?"

"No." His face was turned away from her, looking back at the cages, and she felt his thin frame stiffen. "Lizzie, look . . . the white one is still alive!"

YOSEMITE

LIZZIE TWISTED HER head to follow his gaze and her heart nearly stopped. Inside the cage on the left, Tamarack's ghostly shape shifted. A minute later, the wolf raised her head.

"Oh!" Lizzie cried, grabbing Tyler.

"What's going on?" Tyler whispered. "It's like she's waking up."

Lizzie clutched his arm. "Maybe she's all right."

They stared at each other. "Maybe Lobo is, too," she whispered, almost afraid to let herself believe it. Her heart raced with joy and relief.

Tyler's eyes were wide. "But that means we're back here with two WOLVES," he said shakily.

It was true. The wolves were barely a foot away, their massive furry shapes filling the cages. But Lizzie didn't care. Her eyes were glued on Lobo. *Please,* she thought. *Please.*

And then suddenly she understood. She rolled up on her elbows, staring down at Tyler. "Karen's going to let them go."

"What?"

"She's going to release them! In the park."

Tyler stared at her. "In Yosemite?" he asked in confusion. "But they're sick. Why would she set them free when they're dying?"

"Listen." Lizzie grabbed his arm, piecing it together in her mind. "I wonder if . . . do you think Karen could have been making them sick somehow?"

Tyler frowned. "That would be seriously messed up. She's a vet! She's supposed to make them better!"

"I know. I know," Lizzie said. "But what if she was making them sick just so she'd have a reason to take them out of the zoo?"

Tyler glanced back at the cages, where Tamarack was stirring. "But the white one, Tamarack . . . she wasn't even dead. Couldn't your dad tell that?"

"Sure, if he examined her. But he would trust Karen.

 200

I mean, she's the vet, so he'd have no reason not to. And if they were worried about the disease spreading, nobody would get too close to the sick wolves, you know? That's why my dad wanted an autopsy."

Tyler stared at her. "But if she's doing that, making them sick, that's got to be illegal, right? I mean, she's a vet, and she works for the zoo."

Lizzie nodded, unsure what to think. "But that means Tamarack is going to be okay. And Lobo, too," she said urgently. She couldn't believe it, savoring the flood of relief.

She peered through the rear window at the dark, smooth shape of Karen's head. There was something so unknowable about her. Lizzie remembered what her dad had told her about Karen and Nature Justice, that environmental group she'd been so passionate about. There'd been a story about people getting arrested for trying to protect an old-growth forest. Karen was so strong in her beliefs. Lizzie felt uncertain so much of the time herself and had often envied that quality, but now she realized she was seeing it carried to its logical conclusion: Karen's conviction that what she believed was even more important than the law.

"Are there even wolves in Yosemite?" Tyler asked. "Is it okay to let them go there?"

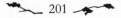

Lizzie shook her head, stunned, her mind still racing. "I don't know. I've never seen one in the park. Listen, Tyler—maybe Athena didn't die." Her words tumbled over one another. "Remember how you saw an animal in the truck a few nights ago? Leaving the zoo? What if it was Athena? And Karen was taking her to Yosemite to set her free."

Lizzie thought about hearing her father talk to Karen the day Athena died, how surprised he'd been that she'd already gotten rid of the body, without any confirmation of what killed the wolf. She thought of that night when she and Tyler had gone to the wolf pen, how someone had bent over Tamarack and done something to her. She had wondered if it was Ed, or even one of the custodians, but now it seemed clear it had been Karen.

"The *vet* is making them sick," Tyler said slowly.

"So she can set them free."

Lizzie didn't even know how to feel. As awful as it was that Karen had given the wolves something that made them so weak and ill, she had done it to free them. To get them out of the pen in the zoo and let them loose in the woods. Where they belonged.

She turned back toward the cages and knew what she would see before she actually saw it. Lobo's huge, dark form moved—once, almost a shiver, and then again. Through the darkness, she saw him raise his head and glimpsed his pale silver eyes.

Lizzie felt a sharp thrill: part fear, part excitement, part pure joy. Lobo was alive!

"Look at Lobo," she whispered to Tyler.

Even in the blackness of the truck bed, she could tell that Tyler was petrified.

"They're in cages," she told him. "They can't hurt us."

"But what about when she releases them?" Tyler said softly.

The words were barely out of his mouth when they felt the truck slowing down, and then bumping and jolting off the edge of the road. Lizzie lifted her head and, over the side of the truck bed, she could see that they were driving across a grassy meadow, with tall trees looming ahead and immense walls of rock rising in the distance. The moon shone on the high cliffs. She knew the contours of the landscape immediately, from a dozen camping trips with her father . . . not just the shape of it, but the particular sound of its silence, the sharp earthy smell of the forest.

"We're in Yosemite," she whispered to Tyler.

They huddled together in wonder as the truck bumped and banged over rough ground.

Chapter 21

WOLVES
IN THE WOODS

"GET READY," TYLER whispered. "She's about to stop."

Lizzie pressed herself flat. The truck had been bumping and jostling over uneven ground. Now it was going more slowly, as grass crunched and rustled beneath the tires.

"We have to jump out. If we don't, she'll see us," Tyler said softly.

He rolled to the side of the truck bed, pulling his backpack with him and balling the blanket against his chest. Lizzie scooted on her stomach next to him. In the cages, the wolves were stirring, clanging against the metal, struggling to stand.

The truck had slowed to a crawl.

"Now!" Tyler whispered.

He lifted himself over the edge of the truck bed, tossing the backpack and blanket over the side. With an urgent look at Lizzie, he tumbled after them, landing in the grass with a soft *oomph*.

Lizzie gripped the metal rim. She was desperate to get out before the truck stopped, but afraid of falling under the wheels.

In the darkness, she could see Tyler beckoning to her. There was no time. She threw her legs over the side of the truck, pushed off with her hands, and jumped.

She hit the ground with a thud, scraping her palms on the prickly grass.

Tyler grabbed her hand and yanked her up. He had his backpack hooked over one shoulder and thrust the blanket into her arms. "Hurry," he whispered. "Run to those trees."

They raced over the rough meadow in the direction of the woods, just as the truck rolled to a halt.

With the engine cut off, they were abruptly subsumed in a shocking silence. Tyler scrambled through the trees and ducked behind a large, mossy rock. He motioned Lizzie to follow him. The truck had stopped just a dozen yards away. After a minute, Lizzie heard the groan of the driver's side door opening, and then

Karen stepped out and walked toward the tailgate. Lizzie could see she was holding something in her hand.

"What's she carrying?" Tyler asked.

"I can't tell from here."

The tailgate clanged down and Karen hoisted herself up onto the truck bed. The clink of the cages rattling carried through the cool night air, and even from a distance, Lizzie could tell that the wolves were moving around. Karen crouched over Tamarack's cage, and the wolf made a sound that was half snarl, half yelp.

Tyler strained over the hummock of rock. "She's giving them a shot," he said.

Now Karen squeezed around the other cage and knelt down next to Lobo. She seemed to be talking to the wolves, but Lizzie couldn't make out any words.

She craned over the top of the boulder, trying to get a better look.

"What's she doing now?" Tyler asked.

Lizzie leaned toward him, tugging the blanket over her shoulders. "I don't know. She's just sitting there."

Karen seemed to be sitting back on her heels in the truck bed, watching the wolves.

Inside the cages, Tamarack and Lobo were growing more and more active. Lizzie could see them fully on their feet now, turning and twisting, banging against

the wire mesh. Tamarack's pale fur glowed in the moon-light. A minute later, Lobo lunged against the door of the cage, his shaggy shoulders so massive that he all but blocked Tamarack from view.

"Look," Tyler whispered. "They seem fine now."

Lizzie could feel the frightened gallop of her heart. Karen stood and negotiated her way around the cages, toward the cab of the truck. Grunting with the effort, she pushed Tamarack's cage along the truck bed to the open tailgate. It scraped loudly against the metal. Then she pushed Lobo's cage next to it, so both cages were at the edge of the open tailgate, facing the meadow beyond. The wolves were whirling furiously, banging against the wire mesh.

Karen leaned across the top of Tamarack's cage and fiddled with the release. Lizzie heard her say something under her breath, and then abruptly, the cage door dropped open.

Tamarack leapt out. Her pale form glided through the air, a comet in the night. She streaked across the meadow, directly toward the woods.

"Watch out!" Tyler whispered. In fright, Lizzie pressed herself against the rough side of the boulder. But the wolf swerved away from them, disappearing through the trees.

They barely had time to catch their breath when they heard the second cage door clang open.

"Lobo," Lizzie whispered. She raised her head just in time to see the big wolf soar over the tailgate, impossibly light and fast and free.

He skimmed across the grass, loping over the meadow. Lizzie braced herself, but Lobo just followed Tamarack's path. An instant later, he, too, had disappeared.

"Stay down," Tyler warned her.

Karen was still crouched in the truck bed, gazing out at the empty meadow. Then swiftly and firmly, she pushed the cages back toward the cab of the truck, jumped to the ground, and banged the tailgate shut. She walked around to the driver's side and climbed in.

"She's leaving!" Lizzie cried. "We have to get back to the truck."

"But she'll see us," Tyler protested.

"Do you want to be left here?" Lizzie countered. "With the wolves? Run!"

Just as they started out from behind the rock, the truck's engine rumbled to life. Karen began driving slowly back across the meadow.

"Hurry!" Tyler urged Lizzie, racing ahead, his backpack flapping against his shoulder blades. She ran after him, throwing down the blanket and stumbling past the trees into the meadow. They ran through the prickly grass.

The truck was far ahead, its headlights casting wide arcs of light over the field. For an instant, Lizzie could see the shadows on either side morph into bushes and trees; big, jagged rocks. Tyler's slim shape darted gracefully through the brush ahead of her.

"We're not going to make it," he cried, and Lizzie could see him slowing down.

As they watched, the truck bounced noisily away from them, gaining speed. Finally, its taillights disappeared, swallowed by the night.

Out of breath, Lizzie leaned over her knees, gulping lungfuls of air.

Tyler had stopped a few feet ahead. His backpack lay on the ground.

Lizzie walked over to him. "What do we do now?" she asked.

He stooped and felt for the strap of his backpack, swinging it into the air. "Get the blanket and then find a place to sleep, I guess."

She looked around at the immense darkness, the high walls of the canyon that sparkled under a sky full of stars. She'd been camping in Yosemite many times, but not like this. Not without a tent, and sleeping bag, and food and water. Not without her father.

Her father! What would Mike be thinking? It was late now, and he had no idea where she was. A day often passed without her seeing him—things were so busy at the zoo, she never even knew where he was most of the time—but always, always, she was there when he came home at night. She pictured Mike walking into the empty house and calling for her in the echoing silence.

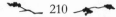

She turned to Tyler hopelessly. "How can we stay here? There's no place for us to sleep."

Even in the darkness, she could sense his jaw tighten. "We'll sleep on the ground." It sounded like a reproach, and of course this was nothing new for him. He'd probably been sleeping on the ground for weeks.

Stung, she watched as he heaved the backpack over his shoulder and turned, walking toward the woods.

When she didn't immediately join him, he stopped and seemed to relent. "Come on, we'll be okay. I know how to do this."

She looked at him dubiously.

"Where's the blanket?" he persisted.

"I dropped it when we ran. But I don't see it now. It's too dark."

"Let's go back to where we were. We'll find it."

Lizzie followed him across the field, sharing none of his certainty. The meadow was a black blur, bordered by the tall, indistinct shapes of the trees. Somewhere in that forest was the blanket . . . and the wolves.

Chapter 22

SOUNDS
IN THE DARK

WHEN THEY REACHED the grove of trees, Lizzie started searching the needle-covered earth for the blanket.

Tyler glanced around. "Where did you leave it?"

"I don't know. Near the rock, I think."

"Which rock?"

"The rock we were hiding behind," she answered impatiently. There were boulders scattered throughout the woods, and it was so dark, Lizzie had no idea which one was their hiding place.

"Maybe that's it." She pointed.

Tyler shook his head. "It was bigger than that."

They walked farther into the trees, kicking at the carpet of needles and fir cones. "Did you pack a flashlight?" Lizzie asked.

Tyler frowned at her. "No."

"That would have been a good idea."

"It would have been a good idea to hold on to the blanket."

"I didn't know we were going to end up spending the night in the woods!"

"Neither did I!"

They stared at each other, fuming.

"It was your idea to get in the truck," Lizzie said.

"Didn't you want to find out what was going on with the wolves?" Tyler demanded. "You were so worried. I did it for you! Now we know they're all right." He turned away from her, balling his fists. "And it wasn't my idea to get stuck here. No way. I would've made it back to the truck if you hadn't been so slow."

"Slow!" Lizzie exclaimed, outraged. "I'm as fast as you are!"

"Well, all I'm saying is, I ran with my backpack. It's a lot heavier than the stupid blanket, but you couldn't handle running with that." He glared at her. "And now we need it! It's cold."

"Then stop complaining and help me find it," Lizzie snapped.

She scuffed at the ground as she walked, hoping her sneaker would hit something soft. All the rocks looked the same now, just big blobs. The trees crowded around, and she wandered through the maze of trunks.

"Are you still looking?" she called.

There was no answer.

"Tyler?"

Now she looked up, searching the darkness for Tyler's silhouette. She didn't see him, and her heart began to pound. "Tyler!"

Frantically, she turned back the way she'd come, scanning the trees for any sign of movement. What if the wolves were here? What if they'd run away from the truck but were just waiting there, nearby in the woods?

"TYLER!" she yelled.

She hurried in the direction of the meadow, where the faint moonlight at least gave some hope of visibility. And then she heard it. A high keening noise. It echoed through the air, rolling over her in waves, chilling her to the bone. A howl.

She froze.

A few seconds later, it came again, a rippling,

building crescendo. The wolves were howling. And then, far away, she thought she heard a high, faint, crooning answer.

"I'm here," said a low voice. She turned to see Tyler at her elbow. He was holding the blanket.

"You found it," she said.

He nodded, but his face was twisted toward the howling, his brow furrowed. "Why are they doing that?"

"It's how they communicate," Lizzie said. "I think they're trying to figure out where they are."

When Tyler looked puzzled, she added, "If none of the wolves were really sick, then Athena is probably here somewhere, too. I think they're calling to her, and she's howling back."

"Then there are three of them," Tyler said grimly.

Lizzie nodded. Three. It was almost a pack.

"And only two of us," Tyler added.

Lizzie nodded again, shivering. "Yeah. So we need to find someplace safe to stay until morning."

She took the blanket from Tyler and clutched it around her shoulders, trying to steer a course away from the high, eerie howling that reverberated through the woods.

They walked deeper and deeper into the woods, until the ground began to slope and they were climbing. There were more rocks here, sometimes high mounds of them. They could no longer hear the wolves howling, but Lizzie was sharply tuned to every strange sound

carrying through the trees . . . the rustle of pine needles, the snapping of twigs, the occasional chirp, trill, or hoot of some night creature. Her eyes darted in every direction, scrutinizing the shadows for movement.

"We can stop now," Tyler said. "This is good enough."

Lizzie hesitated. "I think we need to find somewhere that's kind of protected."

"Well, what about over there?" Tyler asked. He gestured to two enormous rocks that leaned against each other, creating a narrow triangular space underneath that was almost like a cave.

Lizzie glanced around. "Okay," she agreed.

"I'm hungry. Aren't you?"

She was too nervous to be hungry, but she didn't want to say that, so she only nodded, spreading the blanket in the rocky cavern. Tyler set down his backpack and unzipped it. Even though the feast from the snack bar was hours old, a salty, greasy smell wafted through the chill air.

"Hey, your notebook is in here," he said, pulling out her green journal.

The cover was bent from when she'd shoved it inside, before throwing the backpack over the fence of the clinic. "I forgot," she said. "Try not to get food on it."

Tyler rolled his eyes at her. "We don't have room for it."

"Well, we can't lose it. It's my summer homework, remember?" School and home seemed so far away right now.

He pushed it to the side and brought out the remnants of dinner, opening containers and unwrapping foil packages. "Hamburger? Hot dog? Fries?"

Lizzie took a cold french fry and munched it, assessing their supply of food. "We shouldn't eat too much," she said. "We may need it tomorrow."

"Yeah, I know," Tyler agreed. "Believe me, I know about food."

Lizzie glanced at him, but it didn't seem to be a rebuke, just a statement. She picked up a piece of hamburger and nibbled it halfheartedly, still shivering.

"You cold?" Tyler asked. "Put on one of my T-shirts. And we have my old blanket from the zoo."

He dug in the bottom of the backpack and pulled out all his clothes. He tossed a clean T-shirt on Lizzie's lap, and then the tattered blanket that she had washed for him at Grandma May's apartment. That day seemed so long ago to her now, her house so far away. She thought of her father again and felt a pang. He would be frightened, searching the zoo for her.

She wiped her hands on her shorts and pulled Tyler's T-shirt over her own shirt, bringing her knees close to her chest to warm up. "Thanks," she said softly.

Tyler looked out at the dark woods.

"I can't believe I'm in Yosemite," he said. "It smells . . ." He sucked in his breath and thought for a minute. "Piney."

"Because we're in the woods," Lizzie said.

"Where are the big mountains? Where's that place from your grandma's postcard, with the ladies kicking their legs off the cliff?"

"The mountains are all around us. You'll see in the morning. The whole place is a valley. El Capitan and Half Dome and the other cliffs are on the outside edges."

Tyler took another bite of hot dog. "Have you been here lots of times?"

Lizzie nodded. "Camping with my dad, and a couple of times with my grandma."

"Can you tell where we are?"

Lizzie shook her head. "Not in the dark. And probably not in the daylight, either. It's a really big park. I mean, there's a spot in the valley that has a bunch of hotels and campgrounds—it's called Yosemite Village. But I don't know if we're anywhere near that."

Tyler munched a fistful of fries, then yawned. "So look at us—we're kind of camping."

Lizzie surveyed their meager campsite, the worn blanket, the sodden remains of their dinner. "Kind of."

Tyler wiped his mouth on his shirt, then looked at her more closely. "We'll be okay," he said. "We've still got plenty to eat. And there's two of us! That helps."

Lizzie was thinking that meant the food would last half as long, but she kept silent. She thought of Tyler sleeping outside at the zoo, night after night, alone.

"I wish I had a way to tell my dad I'm okay . . . we're okay," she corrected. "He's going to be crazy worried. If only I had my phone!"

"It probably wouldn't work out here anyway," Tyler said, gathering up the leftovers.

"He's probably calling the police," Lizzie added, mostly to herself.

Tyler frowned. "Will he tell them about me?"

"Well, probably. But the police are already looking for you, right? I mean, you ran away a while ago."

Tyler didn't answer, but he began shoving the wrapped parcels of food into the backpack, and thrust a bottle of water at her.

"Thanks," she said, thirsty from the salty food. She took a long gulp and the freshness of the water cooled her throat. When she handed the bottle back, Tyler pushed it into the backpack, tugging the zipper closed with such force she thought he might break it.

"What's the matter?" Lizzie asked. "It's not like the

police don't know you're missing. I'm sure your foster family called them as soon as you didn't come home."

He glowered at her, not saying anything.

"What . . . do you think they *didn't* call the police? C'mon. You've been gone a long time."

Tyler turned away, ducking under the rocky canopy of their makeshift shelter and busily smoothing the blanket. "They have a bunch of other kids," he said. "Seven of us. So sure, they called the police, but it's not like with your dad. It's not like they're really gonna miss me."

"You're wrong," Lizzie said, suddenly sure of it. "I bet they are really worried about you. Aren't you ever going back?"

He was silent for a minute. "Yeah, I guess. Eventually. You think we can sleep here? Under these rocks?"

Lizzie glanced at the place where the two boulders joined, making an upside-down V. "Yeah," she said. "But we'll have to be careful of bears. They'll smell the food."

"Bears and wolves," Tyler amended, scanning the dark woods.

"Right." Where were the wolves? She peered into the shadowy trees. Anything could be hiding there.

She lifted the heavy backpack and walked down the

hill with it, away from the rocks, until she found a small tree. "A bear won't be able to climb this one," she called to Tyler. "Help me put it high enough that it's out of reach."

Tyler came down the slope to join her.

"Here," he said, lacing his fingers together. She stepped into the cradle of his hands and grabbed the rough bark of the tree, pulling herself up until she could reach one of the lower branches. She hung the backpack by a strap, high over the ground.

Tyler squinted up at it. "You think that's safe from bears?"

"I hope so. And if it's not, at least the bear won't be near where we are," Lizzie said.

They made their way back up the hill in the darkness. Lizzie listened to the faint crackle and hush of the woods. It was impossible to tell what was out there. The moonlight barely made a dent through the thick cover of trees.

Tyler seemed to be having the same thought. "Where do you think the wolves are?" he asked.

"I don't know," she said. "Maybe trying to find Athena." She ducked into the rocky archway of their shelter, kneeling on the blanket.

"So now what do we do?" Tyler asked, jiggling from one foot to the other.

"Go to sleep, I guess. Or try to."

She stretched out on the blanket, pulling the other one up to her shoulders. Tyler balled his clothing into a pillow and lay down next to her, covering himself. She could feel the heat from his body forming a warm buffer along one side of her, though they weren't quite touching.

She was exhausted, but she couldn't imagine being able to fall asleep. She stared up at the rocks arching over their heads and listened to the strange night sounds.

"Tyler," she said after a minute.

"Yeah?" His voice was sleepy.

"What happened to your mom?"

"What do you mean?"

"You don't talk about her. Where is she?"

He didn't answer, and Lizzie thought that maybe he hadn't heard her, or maybe he'd fallen asleep. But then his voice drifted out of the darkness.

"She's at a halfway house in Oakland."

"Halfway between what?" Lizzie asked.

He snorted. "It's a place for, like, addicts," he said.

"What's she addicted to?"

He was quiet for a minute. "First it was drinking, then it was drugs."

"Oh." Lizzie tried to think of something to say. "And she couldn't stop?"

His voice was hard. "You can't when you're an addict. Or at least, she couldn't."

Lizzie was quiet. She could sense the shrug of his body without seeing it.

"She cared more about that than anything," he said. "More than she cared about me, anyway."

"I don't think that's true." Lizzie thought of the photograph of his mother, the one he carried in his backpack. She rolled toward him, trying to see his face in the dark. "I mean, when a person is drunk or on drugs, they're not themselves," she said slowly. "So whatever your mom did then, that's not really who she was."

Tyler didn't answer.

"At least she's still alive," Lizzie said.

He sighed. "She was in rehab, but it didn't work. It's like she just kind of faded away." He turned to Lizzie finally, his dark eyes large and serious in his thin face. "Your mom, when she was alive—just for that little bit of time when you were a baby—she was really *with* you. My mom never was."

Lizzie didn't answer. She could hear the hurt in his voice, and she understood suddenly that even though their situations were different, there was this one big thing they had in common: They were both missing something they'd never really had.

She wrapped her arms around her chest, trembling from the cold.

Tyler turned away from her. "Let's sleep back to back," he said.

"Okay."

Lizzie rolled on her side and scooted across the blanket toward him, as he rustled in the darkness, doing the same. He pressed his warm, knobby back against hers, and she could feel his entire story, lying next to her.

She stopped shivering and closed her eyes.

"The wolves are out there somewhere," she said softly. Lobo's fierce, beautiful face rose before her. "What do you think they're doing?"

Tyler's voice was sleepy. "Running and running. Because there's no fence to stop them."

And Lizzie saw that in her mind: the first leap from the truck, the ripple of pure, unfettered energy as Lobo and Tamarack streaked across the meadow. And even though the ground was rough and hard, the air was growing colder, and the wolves were somewhere out there in the night, she drifted off to sleep.

Chapter 23

ENCOUNTER

LIZZIE WOKE BEFORE dawn, when the light was just beginning to change. She had slept in fits and bursts, waking all night long. Twice she'd awakened bolt upright, certain that she heard something moving in the woods nearby. But now that the darkness was turning from black to gray, she could make out the backpack dangling from the tree, so at least their food was still safe.

She stirred a little. Tyler was lying on his back, snoring softly. Her limbs were cold and stiff, but it was much, much warmer under the blanket than it was outside, and she couldn't bear to stand up and face the chilly morning.

Reluctantly, she pushed off the blanket and stretched.

Her stomach spasmed with hunger. She touched Tyler's shoulder.

He jerked, sitting up. "What? What?"

"It's just me," Lizzie said. "Let's pack up our stuff and see if we can find Yosemite Village. I'm starving, aren't you?"

Tyler rubbed his face with both hands. "I'll get the backpack." He stood up, still half asleep, and stumbled down the hill.

"Don't you need help?" she called.

"Nah, I got it," he said. He used a branch from the ground to pull the backpack lower, then yanked it down from the tree.

After a quick, meager breakfast of cold hamburger followed by half of the chocolate chip cookie, they rolled up the blankets, bunched up the clothes, and stuffed everything into the backpack. It was heavy and bulging, and Tyler yanked it over one shoulder with a grunt.

"We can take turns," Lizzie offered.

"That's okay," he said. "It's mostly my stuff." He looked around. "Let's go this way, over the rocks."

Lizzie surveyed the slope. "I think we should go back down to the meadow. Then we can find the road. When a car comes, we can hitch a ride to the ranger station."

Tyler had his back to her, already starting up the hill. "This looks like it might be a trail," he said.

Lizzie could see only trees, with jagged interruptions of boulders. "I don't think so."

But Tyler was determinedly climbing. "C'mon. We'll be able to see better from higher up. Then we can find the road . . . and maybe, what's it called, Yosemite Village."

Lizzie started to protest, but he was getting farther and farther ahead of her. Reluctantly, she clambered after him.

Breathing hard, they scrambled over the large rocks, then made their way over the bumpy ground. The sun was rising now, the sky turning pinkish gray above them. Already the temperature seemed to be changing. Lizzie inhaled the crisp, woodsy scent of the air.

"I can't believe we're in Yosemite." Tyler sounded almost cheerful. "I never thought I'd get to see it."

"I told you we could come camping here," Lizzie reminded him.

"We are camping! Really camping. Without tents or anything."

"Yeah, but we don't have any of the stuff we need," Lizzie commented.

"We have food and two bottles of water. And blankets," Tyler countered. "That's enough." He continued his route up the hill, which was steeper now. The ground had become rockier, with a sheer cliff on the right. The forest began to thin out, and the sky above turned from rose to pale blue.

"Look." Tyler sucked in his breath.

Suddenly, the valley unfurled below them. Massive granite bluffs rose high over the dark pockets of trees. In the distance, a narrow white ribbon of water tumbled down a sheer rock wall, ending in a plume of smoke. A waterfall, Lizzie knew, shrouded in mist at the base.

"Wow," Tyler said softly. "Everything is so *big.*"

"I know." Lizzie remembered feeling the same way the first few times she came to Yosemite. The sheer scale was the most shocking thing—how high the mountains rose above the valley floor, how far the streams dropped from the top of the waterfalls.

"What's that?" Tyler gestured.

"I think it's Yosemite Falls," Lizzie said. "See how it shifts to the left? There's an upper falls and a lower falls."

"Cool." He stared, his face rapt. "I can't believe this is here. I can't believe *we're* here."

"That's Half Dome." Lizzie pointed across the valley to a curved silvery bluff, shining in the morning light.

Tyler turned to her eagerly. "And where's the rock from the picture?"

"Overhanging Rock? I'm not sure we can see it from here." Lizzie shielded her eyes from the sun's glare and gazed out over the valley. "Look," she said. "See those rooftops, way down there? That must be Yosemite Village. We need to go that way."

"Okay," Tyler said. "But can we stay here for a little longer?"

Lizzie hesitated. "Sure. Let's take a water break. I'm thirsty."

They found a flat rock to sit on and passed one of the water bottles back and forth, sipping greedily. Lizzie felt a gnawing worry about drinking so much of their supply—they'd barely started the day, and they had so far to go—but Tyler seemed happy all of a sudden, and she couldn't bear to shatter his reverie.

"Where do you think the wolves are now?" he asked.

Lizzie looked out over the vast expanse of the valley. Lobo was there somewhere. Free! The thought thrilled her, even if it was also frightening.

"Probably far from here," she said, trying to sound confident. "You saw how fast they were running when Karen opened the cages last night."

"Yeah." Tyler glanced around nervously. "That's crazy about the vet making them sick."

Lizzie nodded. It was still so hard to understand.

Karen was intense—she'd been that way the whole time Lizzie had known her—and it was one of the things Mike liked about her, Lizzie knew. But lots of the zoo people cared deeply about animals. It was a different thing entirely to make an animal sick on purpose.

"I mean, she would get fired for that, wouldn't she?" Tyler persisted.

"I guess so." It didn't seem like anybody at the zoo would be forgiving of Karen's deception. "If they figured it out," Lizzie added.

"But then she let them go."

"Yeah." It was the same as stealing zoo animals, probably. Maybe even worse . . . and yet it had seemed so wonderful, so overpoweringly *right*, to see the wolves running free. Lizzie's heart flipped at the memory of it.

"What if she'd given them too much of that stuff by mistake?" Tyler continued. "What if she'd really killed them?"

"That would have been terrible," Lizzie said. "But she didn't. She saved them."

"I know!" Tyler exclaimed. "That's what's crazy. She did this terrible thing, but for a good reason. To let them go."

Lizzie's brow furrowed. "I don't think people at the zoo will see it that way."

"Not even your dad?"

Lizzie thought about Mike, about how hard he worked to make sure the animals stayed safe and healthy.

"No," she said. "Not even my dad. The zookeepers are supposed to *keep* the animals, you know? What she did was dangerous. My dad would say it was irresponsible."

Tyler was quiet, watching her. "Are you going to tell him?"

"I'm not sure," she answered honestly. She couldn't imagine not telling Mike something so important. But then Karen would certainly get fired, or maybe even go to jail. And what if he and the other keepers came to capture the wolves and took them back to the pen at the zoo? She couldn't imagine that, either.

"You think they can survive here?" Tyler asked. "I mean, they're used to being in the zoo, where they get fed and everything."

She looked at him, startled.

"What, you're surprised I thought of that?" He sounded hurt.

"No," she said quickly, "you're right—that is a big problem when they release animals back into the wild." Her dad had told her about the challenges of rehabilitation; the animals had to learn how to hunt, how to identify danger, how to protect themselves. "But these wolves are different," she said. "They weren't born and raised in the zoo. They all came from the wild, and then they were captured because they got injured by cars, or shot at by ranchers for killing cows and sheep. So being in the zoo saved their lives."

Tyler looked skeptical. "If putting something in a cage saves it." He took a long gulp of water, finishing the bottle.

Lizzie said nothing. She screwed the cap back on the empty bottle, staring out over the valley. In the far distance, the curved helmet of rock that formed Half Dome glowed in the morning sun. She thought of John Muir's journals, his rhapsodic odes to nature. Always in his writing, Yosemite appeared as a sacred landscape, almost like a church or temple. In Lizzie's dingy, cramped sixth-grade classroom, it was hard to fathom that, but here, amid the redwood spires and the glittering mosaics of rock, it seemed exactly right.

As if reading her mind, Tyler said, "That cabin is here somewhere."

Lizzie nodded.

"Don't you wish we could find it?"

"Yes, of course," she said. "Maybe someday we will."

"It would be cool to live out here on your own," Tyler said wistfully. "With nobody bugging you, and all this around." He gestured at the valley. "I can see why that guy Muir liked it."

"Me too," Lizzie said. "But I think it would get lonely."

Tyler seemed about to disagree, but then he stood and tilted his head. "Do you hear that? It sounds like water."

"Really?" Lizzie listened to the morning quiet. She thought she did hear something. A low burbling. "Let's head that way. We can clean off, and sometimes there are trails by the creeks."

"I don't need to clean off," Tyler scoffed. "I showered yesterday." But he led the way down the slope, crashing through the brush.

Lizzie stumbled after him.

Late summer was the dry season, a time when the park's smaller streams and waterfalls sometimes dried up. But as they wound their way down the other side of the hill, the rushing noise heightened, and then Lizzie saw the creek. It was shallow but wide, with water swirling over rocks. On the opposite side, two mule deer were drinking. They raised their graceful heads in tandem, and stared at Lizzie and Tyler with moist, dark eyes.

"Hey," Tyler said in a hushed voice, grabbing Lizzie's elbow.

Ears pricked, the deer watched them for a minute. Then they ambled away into the brush.

 234

"Lizzie, look." Tyler kicked the charred remnants of a fire. "Somebody's been here."

Lizzie glanced around. Surely they couldn't be too far from civilization if they'd found a campsite. She stripped off Tyler's extra T-shirt and squatted on the muddy bank, splashing cold water over her arms and face. She shivered despite the warmth of the air. "Hand me the bottle," she told him.

Tyler studied the frothy water. "Is it okay to drink that?"

Lizzie knew there was a risk of parasites but she figured the risk of dehydration was stronger. The sun was high and the temperature was climbing. "We may not have a choice," she said, dipping the bottle into the creek.

When she'd finished filling it, Tyler took it from her and unzipped his backpack to tuck the T-shirt and bottle inside.

"Did you hear that?" he asked. He looked around uneasily.

"What?"

"Something in the bushes."

Lizzie heard nothing but the sound of the water, churning over the rocks.

"Is it the deer?"

"They're on the other side of the creek."

Then Lizzie did hear it, a rustling some distance behind them. "Maybe it's whoever was camping here," she said uncertainly.

Then her whole body tensed. About twenty yards away, poised on the bank of the creek and looking straight at them, was Lobo.

Chapter 24

"RUN!"

THE BIG WOLF stood perfectly still, his silver-gray fur catching the sunlight, the dark streak on his forehead more prominent than ever. His pale eyes bored into them. Lizzie had spent so much time watching Lobo that everything about him was familiar to her, and her heart leapt with recognition. At first, all she could feel was joy—joy that he was alive, that he was free, that he was standing here in front of her. He stared at her with the same steady intensity he'd always had. She remembered the terror of the night at the clinic, when she'd thought he was dead. She took a step toward him.

Tyler caught her arm. "What are you doing?" he whispered in a panic. "Run!"

He stumbled along the bank of the creek, dragging her with him. A huge rock blocked their way, and Tyler scrabbled up the side. Lizzie stopped at its base and turned. You couldn't outrun a wolf. She knew that. Their only hope was that Lobo wouldn't follow.

She saw that the wolf was swiftly crossing the creek, passing as lightly over the water as if it were land. Moments later, the brush on their side of the water rustled and Tamarack's white form appeared. They were together. She crossed the stream behind Lobo, heading through the bushes where the deer had been grazing minutes before. With a shiver, Lizzie realized that they were hunting.

"Look at them!" she said to Tyler.

"They're going after those deer," Tyler said, sliding back down the rock to the ground. He breathed a sigh of relief and looked past her, at the other side of the creek, where the two wolves had disappeared in the foliage. "I wonder what it's like for them."

She turned to him. "You mean to be out in the wild again?"

He shook his head. "No . . . I mean to kill something

and eat it. They probably haven't done that in a long time, you know?"

Lizzie thought about that, the special kind of intelligence and attention it must take for a predator to track and catch its prey. It was a skill the wolves never used in a zoo. And yet everything about them was wired to do exactly that. For humans, it would be like someone who was a great swimmer never being allowed in the water, or someone who was a musician never having the chance to play. It was true for all of the predators in the zoo—the wolves, the tiger, the cougar. In a cage, they could never do the one thing they were born to do.

"Well, I'm just glad they're okay," Lizzie said, studying the opposite bank, where the wolves had vanished.

Tyler swallowed. "If they're okay enough to hunt the deer, they're okay enough to hunt *us*."

Lizzie recoiled. "Tyler, they're not going to hunt us."

"What are you talking about? You already forgot that night Lobo tried to attack us through the fence? There's no fence here." He paused. "We're sitting ducks."

"Oh, come on. Why would the wolves go after us when there are deer around? And rabbits, and all the other animals they like to eat."

"Cuz we're not as fast as deer! Or rabbits." Tyler

climbed over the rocks and started to walk quickly along the bank of the creek. "And could be we're tastier."

Lizzie didn't want to think about that. "That's silly," she said.

"Who knows," Tyler continued. "Maybe they're already hunting us. Maybe they followed us here."

Lizzie frowned into the trees along the opposite bank. "I think they're looking for Athena. You heard them howling last night. I mean, Lobo was staring right at us, and he didn't do anything."

"Maybe he wasn't hungry enough yet," Tyler said. "Hang around and find out for yourself—I'm getting out of here."

He forged on through the tall grass and brambles that bordered the creek. Lizzie trotted after him.

"Hey, wait up!" she called. "I see a sign. There *is* a trail here."

She crashed through the brush toward a narrow dirt path, where a brown wooden sign was posted. In white letters, with an arrow pointing left, it read: YOSEMITE VILLAGE 4 MILES. Beneath that, with an arrow pointing right, it read: TENAYA CREEK 4 MILES, and NEVADA FALL 3 MILES.

Jubilant, she grabbed Tyler's arm. "We did it! We

found the trail to Yosemite Village! Now we can go down there and call my dad."

Her pulse quickened at the thought of Mike. She wanted to hear his voice, to tell him she was all right. "This way," she told Tyler.

She struck out in the direction of Yosemite Village, thinking that four miles would take them a while, especially if the terrain was as rough as this.

Then she realized that Tyler wasn't following her. "What's the matter? Do you want me to take the backpack?" she called.

He was still standing in front of the sign, a strange expression on his face.

"Tyler," she said impatiently. "Four miles is still pretty far. If it's hilly, that will take us a couple of hours."

He was clutching the strap of the backpack, staring at the sign. "Look," he said, tapping it with his finger. "Tenaya Creek."

"Yeah, so? That's the wrong direction."

"That's where the cabin is," he said slowly. "John Muir's lost cabin."

Lizzie walked back to face him, squinting into the sunlight. "Yeah, that's right. One of the places it might be." She tried to read his expression. "We can't do that now, Tyler. We have to call my dad. He'll come get us and take us home."

"Take *you* home."

She stared at him, filled with a new, dawning realization. "Well, okay, but he'll take us both back to Lodisto. And then . . ." Her voice trailed off.

"And then he'll call the cops and I'll be back in foster care." Tyler's hand on the strap of the backpack tightened into a fist.

"Come on," Lizzie said carefully. "It's not like that."

He finally turned to her, and his eyes were huge and hopeless. "Yeah, it is. I'm not going back."

She could read his posture as clearly as she could tell that Lobo had been about to attack that night at the zoo. Tyler was ready to bolt. She stood perfectly still in front of him, as if the slightest movement or sound would frighten him away. "What do you mean?" she said.

"You heard me."

"But Tyler . . . we can't stay here. In the park? That's crazy."

"We were fine last night."

"Not really," Lizzie protested. "We were cold. We were afraid a bear would get our food. And you just finished telling me that the wolves are hunting us."

"And you said they're not," Tyler countered.

"Well, what do I know? You never listened to me before." Lizzie could feel her temper rising. "This is ridiculous. What are you planning to do, live the rest of your life here in the woods?"

"If I have to." Tyler's mouth clamped into a stubborn line. He turned away from her and started quickly up the trail in the direction of Tenaya Creek.

"Well, I'm going to Yosemite Village," Lizzie yelled after him. "And I'm calling my dad. And then we'll get a big search party together and come find you."

"You'll never find me!" He whirled around, eyes blazing. For a minute, they faced each other, both seething. Then he continued on his way, his T-shirt flashing through the trees.

Lizzie felt suddenly furious. She thought of everything she had done for him, taking the blame for the stolen tray, getting him food at the snack bar, giving him a safe place to stay at the apartment. And now he was abandoning her in the middle of the woods? With wolves on the loose? She wasn't even sure she could find her way to Yosemite Village by herself. And he had the water.

She stormed after him. "You're a horrible person!" she shouted.

"Then leave me alone!" he shouted back, stomping angrily through the brush.

"I will!"

"Go ahead!"

"Okay, I'm leaving!"

She strode briskly in the other direction, when she heard him say, "That's what everyone else does."

The anger leaked out of her like air from a punctured balloon. Turning, she saw the slump of his shoulders. He kept walking away from her.

"Tyler. Wait."

He was a dozen yards away now, dappled by the splotches of sunlight sifting through the trees. But he pivoted to face her, his face full of distrust.

"Where are you going?" she asked quietly.

"To John Muir's lost cabin." His voice was firm.

Lizzie sighed. She thought of her own mother, leaving by accident; fate; a thing that couldn't be changed.

Sometimes you had a choice.

She cast one long, regretful glance backward at the path to Yosemite Village and civilization.

"Okay," she decided. "I'm coming with you."

Tyler's eyes widened. "Why?"

She shrugged. "I just am."

"Really?"

She took the backpack from him and slid it over her own shoulder. They started together up the twisting path in the direction of Tenaya Creek.

"What makes you think we'll find it?" she asked.

Tyler grinned at her, looking suddenly much more like himself. "I just do," he said. "We're a good team. I helped you figure out what happened to the wolves, didn't I? Now you can help me find the cabin."

Lizzie sighed, knowing she couldn't leave him. He'd been left too often in the past, and the past was a thing you carried with you all the time, like a burr stuck to your heel. The only way to change it was to create a *new* past, out of what was happening right now.

Maybe she could be that for Tyler: a new past. The one who stayed.

She followed close behind him, as the sun blazed above them and the woods beckoned them deeper and deeper, toward Tenaya Creek.

NATURE'S PEACE

THEY FOLLOWED THE path through trees and dense brush, with the sun hot on their backs. Lizzie felt thirsty again, and it worried her, because they only had one bottle of good water left—and the water from the creek if they got desperate. Now that they were on a trail, she had hoped to see hikers, but the area was deserted. They must be in a remote region of the park . . . which would make sense, she realized. Karen wouldn't have released the wolves near public campgrounds.

The wolves! Lobo and Tamarack had been so close. She thought of the way they delicately skimmed over the water. She wanted to write about it in her journal and describe it the way John Muir would: their feet barely touching the surface, their focus so intent on the deer. But Tyler was right about Lobo. He had tried to attack them once before. And her father had warned her throughout her childhood: These animals were wild. No matter how well you thought you knew them, no matter how strong the bond you'd forged, they were ultimately driven by instinct. Lizzie had heard terrifying stories of zoo animals injuring their keepers. Mike had never shielded her from those, because he wanted her to understand and respect the animals' essential natures.

Mike. What would he be thinking now? It had been a full day since he'd last seen her. He had no idea where she was. She watched Tyler's thin frame bouncing along the path in front of her. Somebody was missing him, too; she felt sure of it.

"How much farther to Tenaya Creek, do you think?" Tyler asked, waiting for her at a bend in the trail.

She joined him, rubbing her face in her T-shirt to wipe away the sweat.

"I don't know. We've been hiking for a couple of hours. It's hot, huh?"

He nodded. "Want me to take the backpack?" Before she could respond, he lifted the strap and she shrugged it free.

"We can rest when we get to the top," he said.

Lizzie felt like they had been struggling uphill for hours, but she followed him in silence as the path zig-zagged up the slope.

"Tyler." She spoke to the back of his head, to his cap of wiry curls.

"Yeah?"

"What happened with your foster family?"

He was quiet, the backpack bobbing against him as he continued up the path. At first she wondered if he hadn't heard her.

"I mean, why did you run away?"

He didn't answer and Lizzie tried again. "Did somebody do something?"

"No! I already told you. It wasn't like that."

"Then what?"

He seemed to be walking faster, and even without the weight of the backpack, Lizzie had a difficult time keeping pace. "I got tired of it there," he said.

"But . . . you had a place to sleep, and food, and people taking care of you," she said. "Even if you were tired of it, wasn't it still better than running away? Having to hide and sleep out in the cold at night?"

"I told you, I like being on my own," he said. His voice was hard.

"Listen, you don't have to tell me if you don't want to. . . . I'm not going to change my mind about coming with you. I just wish . . . I mean, it seems like you wouldn't have run away for no reason, and I wish . . ."

He spun around. "You wish what?" he demanded.

She looked at him, saying nothing. The answer was, she wished they were good-enough friends by now for him to tell her why.

His expression softened. "Nothing happened," he said. "My foster parents, they're all right. They try, you know? But there's a ton of kids, people always coming and going. It's not like it matters whether I'm there or not."

"I'm sure it matters to someone."

"Well, to Jesse," Tyler amended. "But he left."

"Who's Jesse?" Lizzie asked. "Your brother?"

"Foster brother. But he came the same time I did."

"Where did he go?"

"He joined the army."

Tyler turned and started walking again. "So now you know the story," he said.

Lizzie followed in silence, thinking that stories were like that—one detail was a boulder poking out of a creek, with so much more below the surface. People were like that, too, she decided . . . certainly Tyler was.

"Hey, we're at the top," he announced.

The trail turned at the edge of the hillside, about to dip back into the trees, but for a brief moment, they could see the valley again, sparkling in green and brown and gray and silver, stunning in its vastness. The sky blazed above them, and steep bluffs rose majestically all around.

Tyler's whole face lit with excitement. "I could look at this *forever.*"

Lizzie smiled at him. "You sound like John Muir," she said.

"Yeah, I really get that crazy dude now. Why would he ever want to leave?"

"He didn't," Lizzie said. "And when he had to leave, he kept coming back. Wait, hand me my notebook— I want to read you something."

Tyler set the backpack between his knees and fished around for Lizzie's journal. It had a greasy splotch on the cover now, and the metal spiral was stretched and bent. She spread it across her lap and turned to the page she wanted. "Listen, this is something he wrote about Yosemite:

"Climb the mountains and get their good tidings. Nature's peace will flow into you as sunshine flows into

trees. The winds will blow their own freshness into you, and the storms their energy, while cares will drop off like autumn leaves."

Tyler grinned, staring out over the endless landscape of cliffs and forests. "That's what I'm talking about."

Lizzie took a deep breath of the clean mountain air. "It feels like nothing else matters here."

She pressed the notebook against her knees, trying to flatten it. "Know what else John Muir said? That 'most people are *on* the world, not in it.'"

Tyler nodded vigorously. "Yeah, that's right. But here, we're really in it."

They sat for a few minutes longer, feeling fully part of the world. Then Tyler asked, "Do you think we'll find it?"

"Tenaya Creek? Sure, the trail goes there."

"No," Tyler said impatiently. "The lost cabin."

Lizzie gazed out over the valley. "People have been looking for it forever," she said. "Think of all the people who've come to Yosemite since John Muir lived here. Why wouldn't one of them have found it by now?"

"Well, your cousin Clare Hodges did," Tyler reminded her. "Remember the photo? She and that Kitty woman were standing right in front of it."

Lizzie thought of the picture of her cousin standing by the creek, with the faint outline of John Muir's house on stilts hovering behind her. "But that wasn't so long after John Muir lived there. Now it's a hundred years later. More even. So why wouldn't other people have found it?"

"Maybe they didn't know where to look," Tyler suggested.

Lizzie paused. "There are swarms of people here in the summer. Seriously, it's like the zoo. Even the really steep trails have a lot of people on them."

"There aren't people on this trail."

Lizzie saw the longing in his face. "That's true. It's a huge park, so I'm sure there are lots of places people have never been. But . . . well, I'd be surprised if we could find the cabin after all these years when nobody else has been able to."

Tyler shrugged off this logic. "But we saw the photo, right? From your Grandma May's apartment. So we know what the cabin looks like, and we know what that place around it looks like."

"Yes," Lizzie agreed. "And we have my notebook." She ruffled through the pages until she found her sketch and notes, angling the image toward Tyler.

"Hey, that's pretty good," Tyler said, pleased. "It looks just like the picture."

Lizzie summoned the faded photograph in her mind: the ramshackle tree house on stilts, the creek flowing in front of it, and the dense vegetation all around. John Muir's cabin! Where Ralph Waldo Emerson, that man her father had told her about, had been. Could it have survived from the 1870s? What were the chances, really?

Tyler stood. "Come on, it's downhill from here."

Lizzie closed the notebook and slid it carefully into the backpack, trying to protect it from the messy jumble of food. Tyler heaved the pack onto his shoulder, and once again, they started down the trail, which wound along the hillside and then dipped into a redwood grove.

TENAYA CREEK

"HOW MUCH FARTHER do you think?" Tyler asked, after they'd been walking for a while. Downhill was much easier, but the trail was rough, so there was still a bit of climbing required.

"We should be close," Lizzie answered. "The sign said four miles, and it feels like we've been walking a long time."

"Let's stop and have something to eat."

He plopped down on a large boulder and began unpacking the containers of half-eaten food from the day before.

None of it looked very appetizing to Lizzie, but she

was hungry, too. Tyler stuffed the last remnant of hamburger into his mouth and handed her a glutinous pile of damp onion rings.

She took one and nibbled it distastefully. "Isn't it funny how something can taste so different hot than it does cold?"

"Yeah," Tyler agreed. "Anything that's greasy tastes bad cold. Cold pizza . . . yuck. And things that are supposed to be cold, like milk, taste bad when they're warm."

Lizzie thought of him sifting through trash cans at the snack bar and felt bad about complaining. She ate another onion ring. "We shouldn't eat too much," she said after a minute. "Since we don't know how long we'll be out here. And it will make us thirsty."

Tyler nodded, closing the lid of the cardboard box with the onion rings in it. "Maybe we can find some berries," he said hopefully.

Lizzie shook her head. "We shouldn't eat any of those. They could be poisonous. It's too hard to tell without a guidebook."

"A guidebook would be great." Tyler sounded wistful.

"Well, they have those at Yosemite Village . . ." Lizzie said, and then at the look on his face: "Never mind, let's just keep going. We'll figure something out."

Privately, she had no idea how. They were in the middle of the woods, in a park that spanned hundreds of thousands of acres. She remembered her father telling her that Yosemite was the size of the state of Rhode Island. How were they going to find food?

But there was nothing she could do about that now. She shook off her fears and sprang to her feet. "Let's go. It can't be too much farther to Tenaya Creek."

They kept walking along the rough trail, winding their way down to the valley floor. Lizzie's legs ached from climbing, and she was sweaty and thirsty. The path grew flatter, and finally they came to another juncture with a sign that read TENAYA CREEK, 1 MILE.

"We're almost there," Lizzie told Tyler.

"Huh," he said. "That's still pretty far."

Lizzie checked her watch. "It's three o'clock. We just need to make sure we find a good place to camp before it gets dark." The long summer evenings would be a help to them. They had plenty of time before sunset.

"Okay," Tyler said gamely. "Let's go faster." He picked up his pace, notwithstanding the heavy backpack, and Lizzie hurried to keep up.

They were rounding one of the trail's many switch-backs when Lizzie heard a noise down the hill on their right.

She stopped and scanned the slope.

"Did you hear that?" she asked Tyler.

He stopped, too, and followed her gaze. The woods seemed quiet now.

"What is it?"

"I don't know. I thought I heard something move."

Tyler came back to stand beside her. They heard it again: loud rustling, the crackling of branches.

"Is it people?" he asked.

"Maybe." She peered into the trees. She was still surprised they hadn't seen any hikers. But this was a narrow, difficult trail, far from the tourist activity in Yosemite Village, and it didn't appear to lead to any of the park's major sights, like Bridalveil Fall or Half Dome.

The rustling grew louder. Whatever it was certainly didn't care about being heard. Lizzie moved closer to Tyler and nervously searched the bushes.

"Wait . . ." Tyler whispered. "Over there!"

Then Lizzie saw it. Ambling heavily through the underbrush, twigs snapping beneath its feet, was a large black bear. It walked toward them, its massive haunches rippling. It was so close Lizzie could see its broad, flared nose and small eyes.

"What do we do?" Tyler asked, his voice low.

"Shhhh," Lizzie said. "Keep walking. I don't want it to smell the food."

"Will it chase us?"

"I hope not."

There were often problems with bears in the park, she remembered from the times she'd been camping with Mike. They ripped car doors off hinges and broke windows in search of anything that smelled or looked edible, including fragrant suntan lotion. But they generally didn't bother people. She glanced anxiously at the bear. It was still coming toward them, in no particular hurry, meandering sloppily through the brush.

Tyler started walking again, glancing over his shoulder, and Lizzie hurried close behind.

"What if it follows us?" Tyler whispered. "Should we climb a tree?"

Lizzie scanned the tall redwoods surrounding them and shook her head. "It won't help. That bear can climb trees better than we can."

Tyler's eyes widened. "It's still coming. Should we run?"

Lizzie knew how fast bears were—as fast as a horse. "That won't do any good," she told him. "We can't outrun it. If we have to, we can throw it the backpack. That's all it wants."

"No, we can't," Tyler said sharply. "That's all we have."

Lizzie looked back and saw the bear sniffing the air. Did it smell their food? Her pulse quickened.

And then she crashed into Tyler, who had stopped dead in the path.

"Lizzie, look," he whispered. Standing in the woods some distance ahead were the wolves. They stood together with their ears pricked, utterly still. Lizzie wasn't sure she would even have noticed them without Tyler's warning, but now her eyes were riveted on Lobo.

He stared back at her with his steady, unflappable gaze, and Lizzie felt again the spark of connection. Was he chasing her? Protecting her? It was impossible to know. She reminded herself that it was probably neither.

The bear saw the wolves. It rose on its hind legs, its front paws dangling against its massive chest. Tyler cowered. "What's it doing?"

Lizzie's heart thudded against her ribs, the sound of it filling her ears.

"I don't know."

A moment later, the two wolves disappeared into the trees, crossing the trail and trotting purposefully down the slope.

The bear stared after them, then dropped to all fours

and turned its attention to a fallen tree. It began scraping the bark aggressively with its paws.

Lizzie let out a long breath. "Keep walking. We'll be okay."

"Whew," Tyler whispered. "See what I mean? It really is like those wolves are following us."

"Or leading us," Lizzie said. "They're going the same way we are. But there are still only two of them. . . . I hope Athena is okay."

Tyler shook his head. "Easier for us to worry about two wolves than three."

Together, they hustled down the path. Lizzie kept looking back at the bear, but it remained where it was, busily digging at the rotten log.

And then they heard the faint sound of water.

"The creek!" Tyler said. "It must be."

Abruptly, the trail ended, and they were standing at the shore of a wide, shallow stream. The brown water swirled and rippled over rocks, cascading past them in foamy ribbons. A small meadow opened out from the opposite bank, but their side of the creek was clogged with brush and small trees, interrupted by craggy piles of rocks. There was a wooden sign at the end of the path that read TENAYA CANYON, 2 MILES.

"Look, Lizzie!" Tyler said, his eyes bright with

excitement. "Tenaya Canyon—where the cabin might be!"

Lizzie stared at the sign. "But see what it says?" She read the text at the bottom of the sign aloud: *"Warning: Trail ends here. Travel beyond this point is dangerous and strongly discouraged."*

Tyler shrugged. "Yeah, like travel up to this point *hasn't* been dangerous?"

Lizzie frowned at him. "This is different," she said. "It's the canyon that was cursed by Chief Tenaya, remember?"

She took the backpack from him and pulled out her notebook again, thumbing through it until she got to the page with her sketch of Muir's lost cabin. "Look, I copied down the curse. 'Any white person who enters the canyon will die.'"

Tyler punched the air with his fist. "Sweet!"

Lizzie looked at him blankly.

"Don't you get it? It's just against white people," he said happily. "It doesn't apply to me."

Lizzie swallowed. "Well, it applies to *me*."

They stared at each other across the notebook, over Lizzie's pencil image of the cabin on stilts.

"What are you going to do," she asked, "leave me here? I didn't leave you."

"Of course I'm not leaving you," Tyler said easily.

"You'll be fine if we stick together. Nothing can happen to you if you're with me."

That had hardly been true from the first moment she met him, Lizzie thought, starting with the incident in the food court.

But that was so long ago—not in terms of time, but in terms of friendship—that it didn't even seem relevant now. Four days ago, she hadn't even known Tyler existed. How was that possible?

She pointed to the brambly shore of the creek. "Look . . . there isn't anywhere to walk."

Tyler nodded, a smile spreading across his face. "I know! That means nobody's been here. Except, maybe, John Muir."

He looked at her with such a secret, shining happiness that Lizzie's qualms almost faded. What if they really could find the cabin? After all this time! The hidden, historic house of John Muir! But when her gaze shifted to the creek, spilling frothily out of a dense wilderness, she was filled with trepidation.

"Tyler . . ." she began.

"We'll be okay," he told her. "Remember? We're not on the world, we're *in* it."

And he took off along the shore. Lizzie had no choice but to stumble after him.

Chapter 27

WATERFALL

WHILE THE SHORE of the creek was flatter terrain than they'd been hiking, it was so choked with brush and rocks that nearly every step required a decision. At first, Lizzie led the way, but when she got too tired of bushwhacking, Tyler went first. They took turns carrying the backpack, and Lizzie's shoulders ached from the bite of the strap. She noticed that they seemed to be entering the canyon now, with rock walls that loomed steeply on either side.

She thought of Chief Tenaya's curse. What if Tyler was wrong? What if he wasn't safe from the curse . . . or what if he was and she wasn't? But then she remembered that this was where her cousin Clare Hodges had been, so long ago, and near where her mother and father had hiked once, when they were young, before she was born. The thought that she was walking along the same ground her mother might have walked gave her a strange comfort, like a dangled rope of courage.

The creek rushed beside them, thickly bordered by bushes. There were small, secret beds of ferns and little glistening pools. Lizzie felt almost as if they were wandering back in time, into a primeval grove. It was easy to imagine how this place had looked when the first explorers traveled through it. Or when Clare Hodges and Kitty Tatch came here to have their picture taken by George Fiske.

But as foretold by the sign, there was no trail, and no evidence of humans anywhere.

Tenaya Creek became broader, deeper, and faster as they hiked farther into the canyon, which meant that the large rocks closest to the edge were wet and slippery.

"Watch out!" Lizzie warned Tyler more than once, raising her voice over the rush of the water. Her father had told her stories of hikers being swept into the strong currents of the park's many creeks, dashed to their deaths on rocks, or drowned.

"I am," Tyler answered impatiently. "I won't fall."

Twice Lizzie herself stumbled, scraping her palms

on the rough boulders. The sound of the water grew louder and louder, an insistent roar.

"Tyler! Look!" Lizzie pointed. Far ahead of them, through the trees, she glimpsed a waterfall. It cascaded over a cliff, tumbling thirty or forty feet in multiple slender streams. At its base, a pile of large rocks glistened, framed by a dense thicket of low-growing trees and bushes.

"Hey!" Tyler exclaimed, grabbing Lizzie's arm excitedly. "A waterfall! The cabin was supposed to be near a waterfall, right?"

Lizzie thought back to the story of John Muir and his lost cabin. He'd worked at—what was it?—a sawmill, and the mill was near a waterfall. The little, funny-looking cabin had been built on top of the mill.

"But Tyler," she said, surveying the dense vegetation that crowded the bank of the creek, "there's nothing here." There were trees and bushes all around them, and large, wet slabs of rock, but no sign of any kind of house or shelter.

"Maybe it's on the other side of the creek?" Tyler suggested. They both turned to face the opposite bank. The meadow they had encountered earlier was long gone; Lizzie could see only more trees and brush. And there was no way they could cross Tenaya Creek—the water roared past, splashing over the rocks, rushing from a churning pool at the base of the falls.

"I don't see anything," she told Tyler.

"Let's get closer to the falls," Tyler suggested. "Maybe it's hidden in those trees over there, and we just can't see it from here."

He clambered over the slick rocks at the edge of the creek and pushed his way through the bushes. As Lizzie started to follow him, she glimpsed a silvery blur. She froze, her eyes tracking a shadowy, ghost-like shape in the dense underbrush ahead of them.

It took only a second for her to realize that it was Lobo, and that he wasn't alone. Beautiful, pale Tamarack and gray-brown Athena were with him.

The pack! They were trotting swiftly toward the falls, and Lizzie started to call to Tyler—to tell him that Athena was here, the wolves were all together now, they were just ahead—but as she stepped forward onto a rock, her sneaker slid on the wet surface. She tripped, trying to regain her balance, but she could feel herself sliding. She banged hard against the boulder and then fell sideways, tumbling into the creek.

Chapter 28

SWEPT AWAY

THE WATER WAS so cold Lizzie couldn't breathe. It caught her and pulled her, furious and fast, into the roiling torrent. She grabbed desperately at the bushes but felt herself ripped from the riverbank and carried away, bumping over the rocks.

"No!" Tyler yelled. "Lizzie!"

His voice sounded far away. Lizzie struggled to call out to him, but icy water filled her mouth and splashed into her eyes, blinding her. She tried to stay on her back, tried to put her feet out in front of her, but the current was so swift she was powerless.

She barely had time to notice a large rock straight

ahead before her feet smacked into it, and she was caught for a second, suspended at a curve in the creek. In that instant, she thought of the curse. Was this it? Was this the moment she was doomed to die?

Then she was swept into the stream again.

Rocks scraped her legs and water roared over her. She was under it, then on top of it, then whirling in its vortex.

"Lizzie! Lizzie, hold on!" Tyler's voice was faint.

Bang! Her feet hit another rock, and this time she clawed it, wrapping her arms and legs around it and hugging it with all the strength she had.

Blinking through the icy spray, she could see Tyler running along the shore. "Lizzie! I'm coming! Don't let go!"

He crashed through the bushes along the shore, slipping and stumbling over the wet stones.

"Hold on!" he yelled to her. She saw him dig his foot into the ground by a large bush and grab the branches.

Then he leaned toward her, his fingers flailing in the air. "Can you reach me?"

Lizzie held fast to the rock, coughing and spluttering, squinting through the spray at the watery gap between them. The cold stream pummeled her back and strained to pull her free. Her arms and legs ached from the effort of holding on.

"It's too far," Tyler decided, when she couldn't manage to answer. "I'll get a branch." She watched him scramble back up the bank and push through the bushes, whipping around, searching the shoreline frantically.

"Don't leave me!" she cried.

But he disappeared.

"Tyler!" she yelled. *I can't,* she realized. *I can't hold on.* She thought of her father, back at the zoo. He didn't even know where she was. Then she thought of her mother, and her mind slipped deep into the past, to any faint sliver of memory that remained.

Suddenly, it seemed like she wasn't holding on to the rock anymore. The rock was holding on to her.

At that moment, Tyler reappeared, with a large tree branch in his hand. "Okay, I got you. I got you, Lizzie."

He wedged one foot in the rocks and grabbed a fistful of the bush with one hand. The other he stretched toward her, waving the long, crooked limb of the tree.

"Grab it," he told her.

She shook her head. "The water's too strong. You won't be able to pull me."

"I will," he yelled.

They faced each other over the churning water. "Take the branch," Tyler yelled. "I got you."

And because there was nothing left to do, no hope but this one, Lizzie reached out with one hand. She touched the knobby, crooked end of the branch and gripped it as tightly as she could. Then she flung herself into the water.

Chapter 29

SHELTER

AS SOON AS she released her hold on the rock, the water took her, its icy arms whisking her downstream. She held tight to the branch and tried to gain a footing, but she couldn't fight the current enough to reach the shore.

"Hold on!" Tyler yelled. Through the dense spray, she could see him heaving the branch, pulling with all his might.

But the creek was taking her anyway.

As she thrashed in the freezing current, her foot struck something. It was something hard and still in the torrent, something that wasn't moving. Lizzie pressed both feet against it and grabbed the tree branch with her other hand. Tyler gave a great yank, hauling her through the water toward the edge of the creek.

For one suspended second, the cold creek water was all around her, pouring over her shoulders and head, filling her mouth.

Then she could feel the muddy bank beneath her, and Tyler was pulling her onto the land.

She was safe.

Drenched and shivering, Lizzie rolled on her side. She was coughing and spitting, and she couldn't stop shaking.

Tyler crouched beside her. "Are you okay?" He knelt down, pushing her hair back from her face and frantically searching her eyes. His own were huge and worried.

She gulped and nodded, her heart knocking against her chest.

"I'll get our stuff," Tyler said. "The blanket, to warm you up. I'll come right back."

"No . . ." Lizzie started to protest, but he was already running through the woods, upstream, toward the waterfall.

Trying to catch her breath and shivering violently, she lay with her face against the ground. She stared at

the thick tangle of undergrowth, the bottoms of the bushes and trees growing along the creek. She could see the gnarly trunks, the roots pushing up through the ground. And then she saw something else.

Something long and rectangular. It looked like a wooden board, sunk into the earth, stretching out of the muddy bank and into the creek.

Lizzie rose up on one elbow and stared. "Tyler," she called.

He returned with the backpack, unzipping it and tugging both blankets out. "Stay there, I'll cover you up." He began wrapping the rough blankets around her, and the sudden warmth and dryness made her shake even more.

"Look," she persisted. "Over there. My foot hit something in the creek; that's the only way I was able to get to shore. I think it was a board."

Tyler walked over to where Lizzie was pointing. The board was covered with vines and branches, and he crouched down, clawing them loose.

"There's something here," he said, his voice charged with excitement.

Beneath his hands, hidden by the bushes, Lizzie could see not just one board, but a wall of them. They were dark and splintery, half buried in the bank of the creek, some of them extending into the water.

 275

"What is it?" she cried, sitting up and wiping wet strands of hair away from her face.

"I can't tell. Some kind of shack."

"Really?"

"Yeah, look," Tyler said. "We can go inside."

Lizzie struggled to her feet, with the blankets draped over her. She was still shaking so much she could hardly stand.

Tyler ripped one of the boards loose, struggling to hold it up so he could duck under it. "Toss me the backpack."

She dragged it over to him and he used it to prop the board up so he could shimmy under it. He tumbled inside and a minute later, his face appeared at the opening.

"Here, I'll help you."

Lizzie hesitated. "What's in there?"

"Come see."

Tyler pried the board up so she could crawl beneath it. She squeezed through the gap.

It was dark inside, the only light coming from the hole they'd made climbing in. At first Lizzie couldn't see anything. It smelled musty and stale, like wet earth.

"What is this place?" Tyler asked, touching a splintered plank.

"Probably something a hiker built," Lizzie said.

"Like what?" Tyler asked. "A shed? It looks so old."

Lizzie's eyes were adjusting to the lack of light. It was a small space, maybe six or seven feet across, with warped wooden walls and a sagging roof. The last of the afternoon sun streaked through gaps between the boards.

"You don't think . . ." Tyler said, squinting at the rough plank walls.

Lizzie almost laughed. "It's not a cabin! It's barely even a shack."

"But John Muir built his cabin a hundred and fifty years ago, right? So maybe this is what a cabin from the 1870s looks like." He touched the boards again.

Lizzie shook her head at him in the dark. "I don't think so. His was up on stilts, remember? This is almost underground."

"But it could have fallen apart since then," Tyler persisted. "And it was supposed to be on Tenaya Creek. By a waterfall. We're on Tenaya Creek . . . by a waterfall."

He spoke more quickly, excitement pulsing through his voice. "And it was impossible to see, hidden under the bushes like this. It's so close to the creek, it's almost underwater. I mean, some of the boards *are* underwater. No wonder nobody found it!"

Lizzie shook her head. "Stop. It's not a cabin. It's a hiker's lean-to. My dad has shown me these before. People build them for shelter when they're camping. Look, it doesn't have a floor or anything, just dirt. It's probably not even that old."

Tyler glared at her. "You just don't want to believe we could find it."

Lizzie recoiled. "What? Why would you say that?"

"You don't think we're smart enough . . . I'm smart enough." Even in the dark, she could see the challenging spark in his eyes.

"What are you talking about?" Lizzie protested. "Of course I think you're smart enough! You've been living on your own with no grown-ups. You figured out what happened to the wolves, didn't you? You found the way to Tenaya Creek." She grabbed his shoulders and squeezed them, hard. "I know you're smart enough to find John Muir's lost cabin! Even if nobody else could for a hundred and fifty years." She paused and glanced around in the darkness at the softly sloping walls of the shack. "I just don't think this is it."

Tyler sat back on his heels, dejected. "But why not? Why couldn't it be?"

There was something in his voice that Lizzie hadn't heard before, a kind of pleading. And suddenly, it seemed such a small thing, really, to allow him this— the splinter of hope that this really was John Muir's lost cabin.

What was history, anyway, but faith in the past . . . in the story people told about the past?

"Well," she said slowly. "I guess it could be. I mean, there's no way to know for sure."

"Right," Tyler agreed.

"And his cabin should be somewhere around here, if it's on Tenaya Creek."

"Yeah," Tyler said enthusiastically. "That's what I'm saying. I wish we had a flashlight. Then we could really look around."

Lizzie nodded. "Maybe there'll be more light in the morning."

She felt cold and tired suddenly, as if all of her energy had washed out of her in the creek. She shivered under the blanket, wrapping it more tightly over her shoulders.

"You should put on dry clothes," Tyler said.

"I don't have any."

"Take my extra T-shirt and shorts. I'll spread yours over some branches so they can dry overnight."

She hesitated and he said quickly, "And I'll find a rock to prop this board open so we have some light." He scrambled through the gap under the board and was gone, leaving her alone.

Lizzie took down the backpack and the board immediately flopped to the ground, blocking the late-afternoon sun. She peeled off her wet clothes down to her underwear and then felt around in the depths of the backpack until she grazed something cotton, a T-shirt, she hoped. After more searching, her fingers pinched a pair of nylon shorts. She rubbed her skin with the blanket and squeezed her hair in it, then pulled on Tyler's dry clothes. The shirt and shorts smelled like Grandma May's fragrant detergent from the apartment. She wanted to bury her face in them.

"Okay," she called through the slats of the shed. "I'm dressed."

"Hand me your clothes," Tyler said, reaching one long arm through the gap under the board.

Lizzie balled up the wet clothing and thrust it up to him. When he returned, he had a log in his arms, and he wedged it into the dirt to prop up the board, so he could crawl under it again.

Lizzie wrapped one blanket around her shoulders and spread the other across the dirt floor of the shed so they could sit on it. "Did you see the wolves?" she asked.

"What?" Tyler tensed. "Where?"

"No, not now. I mean earlier. They were heading toward the waterfall. All three of them, Athena, too! Lobo and Tamarack found her. I think she was in this canyon the whole time."

"They led us here," Tyler said softly. "To the cabin."

"Maybe they did." Lizzie smiled at him.

"But that means they're here."

"Well, they're outside. And we're inside."

In the little shelter, Lizzie felt safer than she had since they'd come to Yosemite. She opened the backpack wider and sifted through its contents. "Hungry?"

"Sure."

They spread the food across the blanket between them and surveyed their limited buffet. "What do you feel like? French fries? Hot dog?" Lizzie asked.

"Let's split the hot dog," Tyler suggested.

Lizzie ripped it in half and took a big bite of her piece. The hot dog was cold and chewy and the bun was stale, but it still tasted good to her. What a long day it had been.

She watched Tyler cram french fries into his mouth. "I don't know how much longer we can stay out here," she said carefully, steeling herself for his reaction. "We're running out of food. And we don't have much water left, either."

Tyler snorted. "We're next to a creek. We've got all the water we need."

Lizzie shook her head. "If we drink it right out of the stream, we could get sick."

"How come?"

"It has parasites and bacteria in it. There are pills you can put in creek water to make it drinkable—my dad brings them when we go camping—but we don't have those."

"That would have been a good thing to bring," Tyler said.

"Yeah. And a flashlight. And a map of Yosemite. And—" She stopped. "But we didn't know this was where we'd end up."

"John Muir probably didn't have those things."

"No," Lizzie agreed. "But I'm sure he had supplies."

Tyler seemed to be taking his own inventory of what food they had left, but he didn't tell Lizzie his conclusion. Instead, he pulled out her green notebook and handed it to her.

"Read me something else he said. Since we might be spending the night in his lost cabin," Tyler added.

She smiled at him and opened the notebook, thumbing through the first pages where she had copied John Muir's sayings for inspiration. The beginning of the summer seemed so long ago.

She read aloud, *"When we try to pick out anything by itself, we find it hitched to everything else in the Universe."*

Tyler stretched out on the blanket and laced his fingers behind his head, looking at her through half-closed eyes. "What's that from?" he asked.

 283

"John Muir kept a journal, too," Lizzie said. "That quote is from *My First Summer in the Sierra.*"

"Hmmm," said Tyler. "What do you think it means?"

Lizzie thought for a minute. "That everything is connected, even though you may not realize it? Like, if you cut down a tree, you might find that it was the home of a special kind of bird, or that in its shade, a certain flower grew."

"Do you believe that?" Tyler asked sleepily.

Lizzie smoothed out the blanket so she could lie down next to him. It wasn't nearly bedtime, but the light was fading now, and she felt exhausted. "I think I do."

"Even about people?"

She smiled. "Sure. I believe it about us." Then she added, "And it's true of just you. I mean, when you ran away, it's not like everything was the same after you left. There was a hole . . . because you can't change one thing without changing everything."

He didn't answer, and his breathing was slow and heavy. Lizzie wasn't sure he'd even heard her. She took the other blanket from her shoulders and curled closer to him, covering both of them.

For a while, she lay there, listening to the soft, steady sound of his breathing. She didn't feel as scared as she had the first night . . . not as afraid of the woods, or the

wolves. The cabin helped. As run-down as it was, it had clearly been around for a long time, which made her think it was strong enough to protect them. And even if it wasn't John Muir's lost cabin, it felt like it had been left there on purpose, just for them.

She rolled on her side and peered through the gathering darkness at the splintered board. She thought of the people who had been here, the conversations they'd had, the meals they'd eaten. And now she and Tyler were joining that history, their own story seeping into the place.

Lizzie's whole body felt battered and bruised by the day. She thought of the curse, and the creek, and how she'd nearly drowned. She couldn't bear to imagine how sad that would have made her father.

As she drifted off to sleep, she pictured Mike. By now he would be frantic. She was gone, and she was hitched to everything else in his universe. *I have to go home,* she thought. *I have to.*

Chapter 30

HISTORY

LIZZIE WOKE TO faint shafts of gray light sifting through the gaping boards. For a minute, she couldn't think where she was. Then the hard ground and damp blanket reminded her. Tyler was still asleep, his back pressed against her, his breathing deep. She scanned the contours of the shed in the morning light, trying to get a better sense of it. Was there any way it could have belonged to John Muir?

It was so small, and now so dilapidated, it was hard to even tell what it had looked like originally. Tyler was right that the makeshift tree house from the photo could have toppled over. Time and weather could have wrestled it to the ground, hidden it in vines, buried it in the bank of the creek. Now it was just a crumbling pile of boards and earth. How could anyone tell who it had belonged to?

But, she reasoned, it was still someplace historic. It had been here a long time, and someone, perhaps from John Muir's time, had built it. Was it more important if it had once belonged to John Muir? The shelter was just as old, and just as precious to its owner, if it had been built and lived in by someone else.

She squinted at the earthen floor. There was nothing here now, just pebbles and leaves and splintered bits of wood. How would they ever know?

As she lay there, thinking about it, she wondered if knowing was the point. Wasn't it more of a mystery, more of an adventure, if they didn't know for sure who had lived here? If the question still hung in the air, any answer was possible. Maybe this was the very shelter where John Muir had written his journals, looked out at the waterfall and the vast granite cliffs, and made Yosemite his spiritual home. Or maybe some other long-ago pioneer had lived here. When you didn't know for sure, there was a kind of freedom. Anything was possible.

She listened to the distant rush of the creek, and thought about things from the past ... this cabin, and John Muir, and her own mother, and Tyler's mother.

She thought about how the past lingered on and on. It wasn't ever really over. Sometimes the past was just a whisper, a murmur. But other times, the past was a roar so loud you couldn't hear anything else.

Tyler stirred, rolling on his side. She studied his profile. His eyelids fluttered open. He jerked awake. "Hey," he said, rubbing his hands over his face. "How long have you been up?"

"Not long," Lizzie said.

He rose on one elbow, shaking the blanket loose. "It's cold."

Lizzie nodded. "But you can see better now."

Tyler looked around, interested. "It does look really old. But there's nothing left. No furniture, nothing."

"No. Whatever was here is gone."

"Well, it probably couldn't have lasted all this time, you know? Especially if the house fell off the stilts and washed down here. That doesn't mean it isn't John Muir's cabin."

"No," she said. "That's what I was thinking. There's no way to know for sure."

"I mean, there may not be anything to prove it is," Tyler continued. "But there's nothing to prove it's *not*."

Lizzie nodded.

"And it doesn't look like anybody ever found this place," Tyler added. "So we could be the first!"

"It does seem like it," Lizzie agreed.

"So . . ." Tyler continued, his voice warming. "I think we found it. I think we really did."

Lizzie looked into his bright, eager eyes. "Do you think we should tell someone?" she asked. "Since it's a . . . historic discovery and all?"

Tyler considered that for a minute. "We could be famous," he said. "For finding John Muir's lost cabin! It's like finding treasure."

"But to be famous, we'd have to tell someone," Lizzie said.

"Yeah, I know." Tyler kicked off the blanket and rooted around in the backpack, pulling out the last sodden remains of food.

"I don't think we should tell anybody," he decided. "It's enough that we found it. I don't want people to come tramping all around this place, looking at it."

Lizzie bit into a chocolate chip cookie and thought for a minute. "Me neither. It doesn't even seem like a man-made thing anymore, you know? More like it's part of the land."

"Yeah," Tyler agreed, crunching an apple. "Like it's just . . . nature."

"What about the wolves?" Lizzie asked suddenly.

He looked at her, startled. "What about them? Did you hear them last night?"

She shook her head. "No. But what are we going to do about them? Don't we have to tell someone they're here?" She thought of her father. How could she keep such a secret from him?

"No," Tyler said firmly.

Lizzie stared at him. "But they belong to the zoo. They're not supposed to be here on the loose in Yosemite." Even as she said it, it sounded wrong to her. Wasn't that exactly where they should be? Loose and wild in the woods?

Tyler finished the apple, and then the french fries, methodically, one after the other, until they were all gone. She knew he was starving. She was starving, too. "So you want them to go back to the zoo?" he demanded.

She sighed. "No, but . . ."

"Then why would you tell?"

Lizzie realized with all this talk of telling someone, there was an implicit assumption that they would be back in civilization with someone to tell. She wondered if Tyler had changed his mind about running away.

"I mean, what Karen did was wrong," she said slowly.

"Well, yeah," Tyler said, as if that were obvious. "She made them sick! She could have killed them. And then she stole them from the zoo."

"Right," Lizzie said. "And that big new exhibit was built just for them. It cost a lot of money! Now only half the pack is there, and my dad is going to be in trouble for the wolves dying, but they didn't really die."

"Yeah, I know," Tyler said. "But it's done. You can't send them back. Once they've been free like this, and had this different life, how could you ever send them back to how it was before?"

Lizzie looked at him, not sure they were still talking about the wolves. "We can't stay in Yosemite forever," she said softly.

Tyler sighed, not meeting her gaze. "Yeah, I know," he said. "But I wish we could."

"We're almost out of food and water."

He nodded.

"Tyler . . . even John Muir left to see his family," Lizzie said. "And even the wolves have a pack."

He didn't answer, but she knew he understood.

Lizzie rolled up the blanket. When they had everything zipped in the backpack again, they got onto their knees and crawled over to the loose board that Tyler had wedged open. Lizzie took one final look around. She tried to picture John Muir here, scribbling his letters furiously by candlelight, or maybe sitting with a tin cup of tea, talking to one of the famous people who had

visited him in Yosemite. Had Teddy Roosevelt been here? And Ralph Waldo Emerson? The wooden boards held their secrets, giving nothing away.

Tyler crawled through the opening and then held the splintered board so Lizzie had more room. As she squeezed through, he warned, "Don't snag my shirt."

"Are my clothes dry?" she asked. She was crouched on her hands and knees, about to stand, when something bright and flashing caught her eye.

"What's that?" she asked Tyler, pointing to the shallow rivulet at the edge of the creek.

"What?" He squatted next to her.

"In the water. Something shiny."

He reached into the creek, then turned to her, his palm outstretched. In the soft dent of it, she saw a coin.

"Is it a penny?" she asked.

His brow furrowed. "I don't know."

She plucked the coin from his palm and stared at it. It was old and misshapen, caked with dirt. But in the places where the dirt had rubbed off, she could see a glint of silver.

"Can you wash it?" she asked. Her heart beat faster.

Tyler took the coin and crouched over the stream.

"Don't lose it," Lizzie cautioned. "And don't fall in."

He leaned over the water, rubbing vigorously with both hands. Then he wiped it on his shirt, peering at it in the sunlight.

"Hey . . ." he said slowly.

"What?" Her eyes were glued to his face.

"Lizzie. There's a date on it."

"What does it say?"

He looked at her with huge, shining eyes. "It says 1869!"

OUT OF THE WILD

THEY LEAPT TO their feet simultaneously, staring at each other in shock.

"But that means—"

"It could be—"

"It's from the time he lived here—"

Their words spilled over each other.

"That's when John Muir lived at the mill!" Lizzie cried.

"It really *is* his cabin! I told you!" Tyler crowed.

"Well, wait," Lizzie said. "Finding a coin with that date doesn't mean it was John Muir's. It could be anybody's . . . but that does mean someone was here way back then!"

They danced across the bank of the creek, slipping in the mud, shouting with happiness. "We found it!" Tyler kept saying. "We found it!"

"Let me see the coin again," Lizzie said, worried he would drop it.

He handed it to her, and she ran her fingers gently over the cold, damp surface. On closer inspection, it looked like a nickel, except that it was larger and heavier, and very, very old. It had some kind of ornate, striped shield on one side. In faint letters, the words *In God We Trust* arched over it, and the date 1869 was inscribed below. On the other side, there was a large numeral five ringed by stars, and more letters, but they were too worn for Lizzie to read.

"Do you think it's worth anything?" Tyler asked excitedly.

"It's worth a lot to us," Lizzie said.

"I know that," Tyler said impatiently, "but maybe it's worth a lot for real. We'll be rich!"

Lizzie smiled at him. "I think it's just a nickel. But," she allowed, "a really old nickel could be worth something."

"I wouldn't sell it anyway," Tyler decided. "It belonged to John Muir!"

"Where should we put it?"

Tyler knelt on the ground with his backpack. "I'll put it in the special pocket, where I keep important stuff," he said.

"With the picture of your mom?" Lizzie asked.

"Yeah," he said, not looking at her. "That one."

Still in a state of disbelief, Lizzie collected her shirt and shorts from the tree branches where Tyler had spread them to dry. They were a little damp. She folded them together, and he stuffed them into the top of the backpack.

Then they were standing on the bank of the creek, blinking at each other in the morning sun, with the water rushing past, burbling and splashing over the rocks.

"Which way should we go?" Lizzie asked, waiting.

Tyler gestured resignedly back the way they'd come.

"Out of the canyon," he said. "Back to that sign for Yosemite Village." He looked at her. "Right?"

Lizzie took the backpack from him and hoisted it over her shoulder. "Right," she said quietly.

"At least we found what we were looking for," Tyler said.

Lizzie smiled at him. "We sure did."

1869 coin from river

2 cm

Lizzie D.

They walked along the creek, retracing their route as best they could, staying well away from the slippery rocks at the water's edge. The sun was up now, and Lizzie could see the steep walls of the canyon rising precipitously above them. Birds twittered nervously in the trees, flapping away when they drew close. The canyon was silent and empty.

"Do you think we're going the right way?" Lizzie asked once. The shore was so overgrown, it was impossible to tell if they were on the same path or not.

Tyler nodded. "As long as we follow the creek, we're good."

So they kept walking. After a while, they stopped and finished the second bottle of water. Tyler took the backpack from her as the sun rose steadily higher in the sky.

"What should our story be? For how we got to Yosemite?" she asked.

Tyler strode through the brush, not turning around. "We'll say I'd never been to Yosemite. And when your dad saw us at your house, we figured he'd send me back to my foster family, so you came with me here, before I had to leave."

Lizzie nodded. It wasn't so far from the truth. "But how did we get here?"

"Hitched a ride?" he suggested.

"At night? Going to Yosemite?" It didn't sound very believable. "I guess we could say we got a ride to Lodisto, and then we climbed on the back of a truck heading down Highway 40, toward the park." It was one lie after another... *hitched to everything else in the universe.*

"Yeah, that sounds good," Tyler answered. She thought he seemed quiet, preoccupied. She wondered if he was thinking about going back to his foster family.

"So Jesse is already gone?" she said.

"Yeah."

"You'll see him again."

"I hope so." Tyler didn't look at her.

"And we'll still see each other," she said firmly. "We'll still be friends."

He made a noise that was halfway between a snort and a grunt.

She tried to catch his gaze. "I mean it. We will. When you're back home—"

"It's not my home."

"Well, with your foster family. It's not like we won't see each other again."

He nodded, looking doubtful.

"Really, Tyler. I promise," Lizzie said.

"Yeah," he said. "But you never know what'll happen."

"What do you mean?"

He shrugged. "I ran away, so ... sometimes they won't take you back after that. I've never been in the same place for more than a couple of years."

"Well, maybe your mother will come for you—" Lizzie began.

"That's not going to happen."

Suddenly, they heard voices. Just ahead of them, picking their way through the brambles, they could see a man and a woman, carrying backpacks. Lizzie and Tyler froze.

"Look at this," the woman said, laughing over her shoulder. "It's a wilderness! We are so out of our league."

"Hey, speak for yourself," the man responded. "I'm an Eagle Scout."

"You think that'll make a difference when that wolf comes after us?"

Tyler turned to Lizzie and grabbed her arm.

The man snorted. "I told you, it wasn't a wolf. It was a coyote."

"Well, it certainly looked like a wolf—" The woman stopped, staring right at them. "Oh, hi. I'm sorry . . . did we scare you?"

"No," Tyler said carefully. "Did you see a coyote around here?"

"Just one," the man told him. "A big guy, on the other side of the creek. My friend here is sure it's a wolf, but I told her, there are no wolves in Yosemite. She's not used to the woods."

The woman rolled her eyes good-naturedly. "I know what I saw," she said. "And why shouldn't there be wolves in Yosemite? Argh, there isn't even a trail here." She glanced upstream, then looked directly at Lizzie. "Where are you two going? Aren't your parents with you?"

"We kind of got lost," Lizzie said. "We're trying to get back to Yosemite Village."

"Oh my goodness, then I'm glad we came this way," the woman said. "This is not a good place to get lost! We'll take you back to the village with us, won't we, Alan?"

"Sure," the man agreed, then whispered loudly to Tyler, "It gives her an excuse to turn around."

"I heard that." The woman took Lizzie's backpack. "I'll carry that for you, hon. How long have you been out here? Are you thirsty? Hungry? We have plenty of water. Here, have some granola bars and fruit. Alan, give them something to eat." And she began fussing in a motherly, insistent way that Lizzie and Tyler could only be grateful for. It was good to have someone else take charge, good to be taken care of.

"Where did you see it?" Lizzie asked shyly.

"The wolf?" the woman asked. "Right over there." She pointed. "But he's gone now."

"What color was it? Gray? White?"

The woman looked at her questioningly. "Well, I didn't really notice. Gray, I guess. I was more focused on the fact that it was a wolf. A very big wolf."

"Coyote," the man corrected.

Lizzie squinted across the fast-flowing water, staring hard into the tangle of vegetation on the other side. At first she didn't see anything, just the trees and the dense foliage of the bushes growing close to the creek. And then she did. Hidden behind a cluster of leaves and branches, she glimpsed two glowing silver eyes.

She sucked in her breath, standing perfectly still. Everything fell away then: the creek, the trees, the other hikers, and even Tyler. It seemed like she and Lobo were the only two creatures left in the world. She stood watching him, steadily, feeling the thrill of his freedom pulse through the air between them. She thought of all the other times she'd stared at him, through the wire mesh of the fence at the zoo. She wondered if she would ever see him again.

Inside her head, she whispered good-bye.

The woman was standing next to her now. "Do you see him?"

"No," Lizzie said. "I think he's gone."

She turned back to the group and they continued along the shore together, on their way to civilization.

Chapter 32

HOME

AT THE RANGER Station in Yosemite Village, Lizzie and Tyler sat next to each other on a hard wooden bench, waiting for the arrival of Mike and Tyler's foster mother. There had been much commotion as soon as they told the ranger their names. The local police departments had received an all-points-bulletin about Lizzie's disappearance two nights ago, and they'd been looking for Tyler for weeks, ever since he ran away from his foster home. The ranger had put Lizzie on the phone with Mike briefly, and she had heard such a flood of worry and relief in his voice that she promptly burst into tears.

"It's okay, Dad," she'd mumbled between sobs. "I'm fine, really." But inside her stomach, a cold knot formed. She felt like she had betrayed Mike by running away, and now she was betraying Tyler by going home. Tyler's hands were clenched on his lap, and she could feel his leg jiggling next to her. He'd withdrawn into silence as soon as the ranger telephoned his foster family, an hour ago.

She wanted to say something to reassure him. She wanted desperately to tell him that nothing would change—he could come to the zoo, stay at her house, still be her friend. But she knew he wouldn't believe that. She wasn't sure she believed it herself.

"You kids thirsty?" The ranger was just handing each of them a can of soda when a blustery red-haired woman burst into the room.

"Tyler! Tyler!" she shrieked, grabbing him from the bench and engulfing him in her arms. "Honey, we were so worried about you!" She held him back to look at him, then hugged him again. "I prayed to God you were all right, and look, my prayers have been answered. Oh my goodness. Tyler, honey."

Lizzie stared at her in shock. Somehow, she'd imagined that Tyler's foster mother would be cold and hard. But this woman was all emotion, and acting just like a real mother. She pressed Tyler's head against her bosom and covered his dark curls with kisses. Tyler looked at the floor and didn't say anything.

"Thank you, Officer," the red-haired woman gushed, blinking back tears. "Thank you for finding him!"

"I'm a ranger, ma'am, not a police officer," the park ranger said. "But we have notified the local law enforcement agencies."

"Thank you, thank you," Tyler's foster mother repeated. "We're just so grateful. We thought we might never see him again. Tyler, honey, come on, let's get in the car. You must be starving, and I know you need a shower."

As she hustled Tyler out of the ranger's office, he glanced back once at Lizzie. She instinctively leaned toward him, but before they could say anything to each other, he was gone.

The door closed with a bang.

Lizzie sat in stunned silence on the bench. Was that it? After all they'd been through? She hadn't even had a chance to tell him good-bye.

And then the door swung open and it was Mike. She leapt from the bench into his arms. The feel of his shoulder against her face, the warm, familiar smell of him, the tight, hard band of his arms around her back— she felt suddenly, irrevocably safe. She clung to him, trying to stop the shudders that rippled through her body.

"Lizzie, Lizzie, Lizzie," he was saying into her hair. "You have to promise me you will never do that again."

"I won't," she cried. "I promise. I'm so sorry, Dad."

On the ride back to the zoo, she tried to stick to the story she and Tyler had discussed.

"I blame myself," Mike said, shaking his head angrily. "You're alone too much. You're always so responsible, I've come to count on that . . . and I forget you're just a kid."

"It's not your fault," Lizzie said, horrified. "You didn't do anything wrong. It was just—Tyler—"

"But who is this kid? Why would you run away with him? And to *Yosemite*? It doesn't make sense."

"I met him at the zoo," Lizzie explained. "It turns out he's been living there, behind the elephant house, for a couple of weeks."

"What?" Mike gripped the steering wheel. "And nobody saw him?"

"No. And I couldn't tell you, I really couldn't, because he didn't want to go back to his foster family. His real mom, well, she's been on drugs and she was sent away, and he doesn't know where his dad is, and he's been in a bunch of foster homes—"

"But that doesn't have anything to do with you," Mike protested.

"Yes, it does," Lizzie contradicted. "He's my friend."

"You just met him."

"I know. But now we're friends." She turned to Mike urgently. "And I have to see him again. I have to. I told him I would."

Mike's mouth clamped into a thin line. "Lizzie, you ran away with him! I'm not sure he's the best kid for you to spend time with."

"He is! He is the best kid," Lizzie protested.

"You could have been hurt, or worse," Mike said. "And what were you doing in the apartment? I saw the groceries, the bed. How long was he staying there? I still don't understand why you ran away to Yosemite. I mean, I know you were upset about the wolves dying. I figured you found out about Lobo and just took off."

He shot her a glance and Lizzie didn't say anything. The story he was telling made more sense than her own.

"I know how much Lobo meant to you," he continued. "But Lizzie, there was nothing I could do."

She heard the pain in his voice and reached over to touch his arm. It was so hard not to tell him! She would have to, at some point, she realized. She'd have to figure out a way to let him know the wolves were all right. But

she couldn't risk that they'd be recaptured . . . and what if something she said meant that Karen went to jail?

Lizzie leaned back against the soft car seat and stared out the window, watching the wooded hills give way to dusty fields. They were already out of the mountains. She thought about Tyler at home with his foster family.

She said quietly, "We shouldn't have run away like that."

Mike glanced over at her, his brow furrowed. "Lizzie . . . you're all I have in this world. Do you understand that? The only thing that matters. If anything happened to you—"

"I know."

She could feel the cold depth of her betrayal. She and Mike were a team. They had been since before she could remember. He needed to know he could rely on her, the way she needed to be able to rely on him. But what about Tyler? Tyler needed someone he could rely on, too.

"Tyler doesn't have anybody," she said in a small voice.

"He has his foster family," Mike countered.

"He ran away from them," Lizzie said. "It's not the same."

They rode in silence then, and Lizzie watched the dry, grassy fields roll past. "How are the rest of the wolves doing?" she asked suddenly.

"Better," Mike said. "None of the others have gotten sick. But . . ." He hesitated. "I had to fire Karen."

Lizzie stared at him. "What? Why?" she asked carefully.

"Well, she knew what we had to do when Lobo and Tamarack died. I'd scheduled autopsies. It was important. I've had the board breathing down my neck ever since Athena died. And instead, well, she destroyed the bodies. She said she did it to prevent the disease from spreading, but something isn't adding up."

"You *fired* her?" Lizzie was shocked.

"Well, I let her go," Mike corrected. "Something's going on with her. She's not thinking clearly, and I feel like she was lying to me." He seemed to be talking to himself now.

"Did you ask her about it?" Lizzie said, watching his profile.

"I tried to, but she wouldn't tell me anything." He paused. "And truthfully, I think I'd rather not know. It'll change the way I feel about her. Anyway, I can't have her making bad decisions when it comes to the animals. There's too much at stake. Now we'll never know what was wrong with the wolves."

Lizzie was silent, relieved that even her father didn't always want to know the truth. "Is there a new pack leader?" she asked, wanting to change the subject. She was afraid if they kept talking about Karen, she would give too much away.

He glanced at her again. "Well, they're trying to figure things out. There's been a lot of fighting since we lost Lobo." Lizzie knew that wolf packs were so firmly structured around hierarchy that as soon as a member was lost—or in the zoo, even just absent for a few days, for medical reasons or breeding purposes—the entire pack rearranged its power dynamic. Since Lobo was the pack leader, his absence must have created even bigger shock waves.

"What are you going to do?" she asked.

"We've gone from seven to four," Mike said. "I'd call it a failed experiment. It's the nicest exhibit space we've got, and people love watching them, that's for sure . . . but it's not working out. I've been talking to a wolf rehabilitation center in Oregon."

Lizzie turned to him. "You have?"

"Yeah. I have a board meeting on Tuesday night and I'm going to suggest we relocate the wolves and use that space for the Siberian tiger instead."

"It would be great," Lizzie said fervently, "to move him from that awful cage."

Mike nodded. "I think it's a good solution. We can

get a female on loan from the San Diego Zoo, and if we have a good facility, big enough, with the right features, we might be able to start a breeding program. Maybe that would make up for the disaster with the wolves."

Lizzie pressed her sneakers against the dashboard, picturing the big male tiger in Wolf Woods, with so much more space, and the cover of trees and bushes, and rocky ledges to climb on. "I think that would be amazing," she said happily. "And for the wolves, too! Could they release them in the wild?"

"Well, that's a process. It has to be done carefully," Mike said. "But eventually, yes." He was looking at her in surprise. "I thought you'd be disappointed. You've spent so much time over there."

Lizzie sighed. "Lobo was the only one I really got to know. And he's . . . he's gone now." She was quiet for a minute. "I want the wolves to be free, out in the wild. Where they belong."

"Yeah," Mike agreed. "Me too."

Finally, they pulled up to the back gate of the zoo and rattled down the long drive to the yellow house, with its big, welcoming front porch. Lizzie felt a flood of happiness at the sight of it, and then a pang when she thought of Tyler. She glanced up at the apartment over the garage and turned to her father with a start.

"How come the apartment windows are all open?"

But before he could answer, the side door to the garage swung wide and out came Grandma May.

Lizzie gasped, flinging herself from the car before it had even stopped moving. "Grandma May! You're here!"

Grandma May hurried across the driveway. She pulled Lizzie into her arms. "Of course I am! When your father told me you were gone, I came right away. I told him, we can't lose our girl. We can't ever lose our girl."

She hugged Lizzie tightly against her, and the only thing Lizzie could think, with a long, wondering sigh, was how happy and lucky she was to be home.

Chapter 33

A VISITOR

LIZZIE COULD BARELY contain her excitement. She was sitting on the front porch steps, tapping her sneakers impatiently against the boards, looking down the driveway. Grandma May had been there a week—the most wonderful week—full of quiet, early-morning walks through the zoo, with the dew sparkling on the flowers and the animals restless and alert; then card games or movies during the hot afternoons; and finally, long evenings spent at the kitchen table, talking and laughing over bountiful dinners. Mike remarked that he had never eaten so well in his life, which Lizzie thought an exaggeration, and slightly resented, since they cooked good meals on their own, in her opinion. But she had to admit, it was nice to be fed and cared for. Grandma May made pork chops, roast chicken, salmon fillets, lasagna, and endless soups and casseroles, each more delicious than the last. Just this morning she had baked a three-layer carrot-coconut cake with cream cheese frosting, and now it sat on the edge of the kitchen counter, waiting for their guest to arrive.

Tyler was coming this afternoon! Lizzie could hardly wait. She had talked to him twice on the phone since Yosemite, and truth be told, both times had felt strained and awkward. She'd called him at night, and she could always hear a lot of commotion in the background, the sounds of people moving around and talking, laughter, interruptions. Tyler had seemed quiet and subdued.

"How is it?" she'd asked.

"Okay," he'd said.

"Do you miss Jesse?"

"Yeah."

What she really wondered was whether he missed *her*, but she knew he couldn't answer, and then she'd feel foolish for asking.

Now, though, he was coming over. To spend the night! All week, Lizzie had been telling Mike and Grandma May about Tyler, how smart and funny he was, how brave he'd been at Yosemite, how he'd pulled her out of the creek and saved her life. After that, it hadn't taken much begging on Lizzie's part for Mike to agree that Tyler could come for a sleepover. But because he had so recently run away, Mike thought that proposition had to be handled cautiously. He'd told Lizzie he wanted to meet with Tyler's foster mother first and make sure she was comfortable with the plan. So Mike had gone after lunch to get Tyler, and Lizzie had stayed behind with Grandma May, helping to frost the carrot-coconut cake. Now she sat on the porch steps waiting for the car to pull into the driveway, nervously jiggling her toes against the boards.

Grandma May came out to join her, settling into the white wicker porch swing and drifting gently back and forth. She plumped the floral cushions and beckoned to Lizzie, saying, "I am looking forward to meeting this Tyler. He sounds like a very interesting young man."

"Oh, he is!" Lizzie exclaimed. "He figured out how to live here at the zoo on his own."

"Yes, that's what you told us. Behind the elephant house! Which sounds quite uncomfortable to me, but I suppose at his age, I would have been more adventurous."

"Well, he was really happy when he got to stay in the apartment," Lizzie said, remembering Tyler's joy at the

pleasures of a hot shower and her grandmother's comfy bed. "He acted like it was a luxury hotel or something."

Grandma May sighed. "I almost feel bad that he can't stay there tonight."

"Oh, don't worry," Lizzie said. "We made up the spare bed for him in the house. And he'll be excited to meet you! I told him so much about you when we were looking at all those old pictures of Yosemite."

Grandma May shook her head. "I still can't believe you were in Yosemite all by yourself, for two nights, with no tent or sleeping bags, and wild animals all around." Her eyes widened in amazement. "You are the zookeeper's daughter, through and through."

Lizzie smiled. "Does that seem like something my dad would do?"

Grandma May laughed. "Not your dad, Lizzie. Your mom."

Lizzie stared at her. Whenever people called her the zookeeper's daughter, she always thought they meant her dad. And probably they did. But of course her mother had been a zookeeper, too.

"We have so many fearless women in our family," Grandma May continued. "Bold, strong women. I certainly don't want you running away again, but I am glad to see you're carrying on the tradition."

"I don't think I would have been so brave without Tyler," Lizzie said.

"Maybe not," Grandma May said. "But I doubt he would have been so brave without you."

That was true, Lizzie decided. When they were most afraid, they'd helped each other to be strong.

Just then, Mike's car rolled down the driveway, and Lizzie leapt up and ran to meet it. Tyler opened the door on the passenger side and climbed out, the old familiar backpack dangling from one hand. As Lizzie raced toward him, he hung back, seeming shy. But she couldn't stop herself. She threw her arms around him, hugging his bony shoulders.

"I can't believe you're here! Come on, come with me; you have to meet Grandma May." She grabbed his wrist and dragged him toward the porch, where Grandma May had risen to greet him.

"Tyler, I'm so happy to finally meet you," she said, taking his hand in both of hers. "Lizzie hasn't stopped talking about you."

Tyler smiled sheepishly. "I'm glad to meet you, too. I like all those old pictures you have." He gestured toward the upper windows of the garage apartment.

"Well, why don't we have a snack, and then we'll walk over there and look at them together?"

Grandma May led him into the kitchen as Mike parked the car.

Lizzie hesitated on the porch, waiting for her father. "So he can really spend the night? He doesn't have to go back till tomorrow?" she asked anxiously.

Mike grinned at her. "Better than that. If everything goes okay, he can spend the whole weekend."

"Seriously?"

Mike nodded. "They have their hands full over there, and it's fine with them. We'll see how it goes, but I don't have any problem with him spending weekends here if you guys would like that. We have plenty of room."

"Really, Dad?" Lizzie thought she was going to burst. "That would be awesome!"

"Don't say anything yet," Mike told her. "Let Tyler get settled and then we'll see if that's something he wants. But honestly, I'd rather have you both here, where I can keep an eye on you."

"Okay," Lizzie said, but she was sure it was something Tyler would want.

In the kitchen, Grandma May was slicing thick wedges of carrot-coconut cake and putting them on plates.

Tyler looked at the cake skeptically. "Carrot?" he asked.

"It doesn't taste like vegetables," Lizzie reassured him.

He sniffed it. "Smells good," he said.

"I hear you rescued my granddaughter from a raging torrent," Grandma May said, handing him a heaping plate.

"The creek," Lizzie explained.

Tyler sat at the table, sampling a forkful. "Hey, this is pretty tasty," he said in surprise. "Yeah, she fell in the creek and I had to pull her out." He shrugged nonchalantly.

"And weren't you soaking wet?"

"We had blankets with us," Lizzie said. "And I wore Tyler's extra clothes." She turned to him. "I have them for you upstairs."

"But then you had to spend the night!" Grandma May said. "Weren't you cold?"

"Well, we found a . . ." Tyler stopped, looking at Lizzie, and the secret shivered in the air between them.

"Kind of a hiker's lean-to," Lizzie said. "Old and fallen down, but it was something. We crawled in there."

"And where were you in the park?" Grandma May asked. "Which creek?"

"Tenaya Creek. In Tenaya Canyon," Lizzie said.

"Can you believe that?" her father asked Grandma May incredulously. "Tenaya Canyon! One of the most dangerous areas of the park."

"Because of the curse," Lizzie said. "But we figured the curse was just on white people. So Tyler would be okay."

"And I was!" Tyler added enthusiastically. "Lizzie fell in the creek, but I was fine."

"Great," Mike said.

"Well, it was great," Lizzie pointed out, "because that's why he was able to rescue me."

Finished with the cake, Tyler stood up and licked

frosting off his fingers. "So can we go over to the apartment now? To look at the old pictures?"

"Of course," Grandma May told him. "Lizzie, why don't you show Tyler where he'll be staying and he can leave his backpack there."

Lizzie led Tyler upstairs to the guest room, which was next to her bedroom. It doubled as her father's study, so it had a twin bed against one wall next to a desk and two big bookcases. Tyler sat on the edge of the bed and bounced.

"Cool," he said. He looked out the window. "I can see the apartment from here."

Lizzie smiled. "And over there if you look hard, you can see the elephants." Past the rooftop of the garage, on a hill behind some trees, was the elephant house. In the distance, the gray backs of the elephants moved through the bushes, dappled by sunlight.

"I can't believe you're here," Lizzie said.

He grinned at her, and for the first time, he looked fully himself. "Me neither. I thought I'd never see you again."

"I told you!" Lizzie protested. "I said we'd still be friends."

He shrugged, still smiling. "Yeah, I know. But I didn't believe you."

"Do you still have the coin?" she asked.

"Sure I do. It's still in my backpack pocket." She felt again the thrill of finding it in the shallows of Tenaya Creek.

They ran downstairs to Grandma May, and then the three of them walked across the yard to the apartment.

"I have something to show you," Grandma May said as she climbed the narrow stairs to the second floor.

"What?" Tyler asked. "Another Yosemite photo?"

She smiled at him, raising her eyebrows. "Even better."

In the bright little living room, the sun poured through the windows, and Grandma May sat on the couch. Tyler sat next to her, and Lizzie knelt on the floor at her feet. Grandma May leaned over to the cupboard under the bookshelf and took out the folder of Yosemite photos that Lizzie and Tyler had found.

She held up a tattered, brownish square of paper, covered in faded cursive handwriting. "I discovered this when I was going through some files at my house. I brought it with me when I came."

"What is it?" Lizzie asked.

Tyler leaned closer for a better look.

"It's a letter to . . . Jeanne? Is that what it says?"

Grandma May nodded cryptically. "Jeanne Carr. A friend of John Muir's."

Tyler bounced forward excitedly. "Who's the letter from?" he demanded.

"Who do you think?" Grandma May asked.

"Not . . . John Muir," Lizzie whispered. "But how do you have it?"

"I think cousin Clare must have gotten it somehow. From one of her friends in Yosemite. Jeanne Carr visited the park many times."

"What's it say?" Tyler asked.

Grandma May held it to the light. She read aloud:

Dear friend Mrs. Carr,

Fate and flowers have carried me to California, and I have reveled and luxuriated amid its plants and mountains nearly four months. I am well again, I came to life in the cool winds and crystal waters of the mountains, and, were it not for a thought now and then of loneliness and isolation, the pleasure of my existence would be complete.

Grandma May paused and scanned the creased and fragile paper. She continued reading:

Strange and beautiful mountain ferns, low in the dark cañons and high upon the rocky, sunlit peaks,

banks of blooming shrubs, and sprinklings and gather-
ings of flowers, precious and pure as ever enjoyed the
sweets of a mountain home. And oh, what streams are
there! Beaming, glancing, each with music of its own,
singing as they go in the shadow and light, onward
upon their lovely changing pathways to the sea.

Lizzie closed her eyes, listening to the sound of her
grandmother's voice. She pictured the crooked tree
house on stilts, the one in the photo, and the roaring
waterfall and creek winding beside it. She imagined
the fallen-down shack where she and Tyler had spent the
night. She glanced over at Tyler and smiled.

"Wow, he has a lot to say," Tyler commented.

"Yes, it's very descriptive, isn't it?" Grandma May
held out the letter for them to see. "And this is only a
small part of it! You can really picture what it was like
for him in the mountains."

Lizzie thought of the park's tall redwoods and
shining granite bluffs, the cool stillness of the morning air.

"I had an idea," Grandma May continued. "I'm here
for another week. What if we go to Yosemite together?"

Tyler's face broke into a slow grin. "For real?"

Grandma May laughed. "Yes! We could stay at the

Ahwahnee Hotel and go hiking. Maybe we could even look for John Muir's lost cabin."

"Sure," Tyler said, nodding vigorously. "Now that we know our way around the place." He turned to Lizzie with shining eyes. "I didn't think I'd ever get to go back," he said softly.

Lizzie wrapped her arms around her knees and rocked backward, beaming up at her grandmother. "That's a great idea," she said. "With my dad, too."

And in the sunny little apartment, with Tyler and her grandmother sitting next to her, Lizzie imagined returning to Yosemite, to the woods and streams and mountains . . . and to the wolves, there in the beating heart of the wild.

TREE HOUSE

LIZZIE LED THE way up the ladder and crawled across the rough plank floor. "See? My dad finished it last night," she called down to Tyler.

The tree house had been their project for the rest of the summer, and Tyler and Lizzie had spent hours working on it with Mike almost every weekend. Just the day before, Mike had done a final safety check, making sure all the nails, boards, and screws were secure. So here it was, finished, and just in time, too—unbelievably, school was starting next week.

Lizzie scrambled to her feet and peered through the leaves at the quiet yard below. She could see the sloping roof of the garage apartment, and in the distance, the colorful, busy contours of the zoo. There was the lake with the flamingos; near it, the pasture with the gazelles and giraffes. Paths bordered by bright drifts of flowers wound through the network of animal compounds, and throngs of people meandered along, pushing strollers, holding hands, stopping to stare at the animals.

Tyler bobbed up beside her, his face glowing with approval. "Sweet!" he said. "You can see everything from here." He stepped onto the lowest slat of the railing and balanced, pointing. "Look, the elephants!"

Lizzie climbed up next to him. "You can even see the otters."

For a minute, they hung there, suspended in place and time, hovering in the treetops. Lizzie could see the world spread out below like a colorful patchwork of past and future.

"This tree house," Tyler said. "It's like John Muir's cabin—don't you think? The house on stilts?"

That old photograph was the very thing that had inspired the plan. She nodded. "It is."

"Then it would be a good place for this." Tyler buried his hand in his shorts pocket, then held something out in his palm.

She knew what it was before she even looked. She

smiled at him. "Where can we put it to keep it safe?" she asked, taking the coin. She held it up to the light, so she could see again the date 1869 engraved in the silver.

"Let's figure out a hiding place," Tyler said, "where nobody else will find it." He surveyed the board floor of the tree house. "Here!" he cried suddenly. In one corner, there was a complicated knot in the wood, almost a divot. He wedged the coin into it and looked at her triumphantly.

"You sure it won't fall out?" Lizzie asked.

"Yeah, look. And it's even covered by the wood, so it won't get rained on."

"Then that's a good place for it."

"Now this tree house really is like the cabin," Tyler said. "And you know what? If it falls apart a hundred years from now, and all that's left is a pile of boards, then maybe somebody will find this old nickel and think our tree house was built in 1869!"

He looked so pleased at this idea that Lizzie laughed.

"I'm going to come up here to write in my journal, the way John Muir did," she told him, gesturing to her green notebook. She'd tucked it in the opposite corner of the tree house, on top of an old blanket.

Tyler walked over to it. "You still writing in that thing?"

Lizzie nodded shyly. "Yeah."

"Am I in there?"

She looked at him. "What do you think?"

Now he laughed too. "I bet I'm all over it."

He bent and picked up the notebook. For a second, Lizzie stiffened, afraid he was going to read it. But Tyler only handed it to her, still grinning.

"Know what? You should hold on to this. Cuz when you grow up, maybe you'll publish it! You know, turn it into a real book, like John Muir did."

"Maybe I will," Lizzie said.

They sat together on the sun-speckled floor of the tree house, staring at ruffled pages of the notebook, which had traveled with them deep into the wilderness, and then out again.

"If you did make it into a book, what would you call it?" Tyler asked.

Lizzie thought for a minute.

"*The Wolf Keepers*," she said.

And that is what she did.

AUTHOR'S NOTE

Readers who are familiar with my other books, such as *Shakespeare's Secret* and the Superstition Mountain trilogy, know that it's very hard for me to resist a good historical mystery! The one at the heart of this story is the mystery of John Muir's lost cabin, his home in Yosemite from 1869 to 1871.

While the present-day characters in this book are entirely the products of my imagination (as are the John Muir Wildlife Park and the town of Lodisto, California), the historical characters are all based in fact. John

John Muir at Mirror Lake, c. 1902 [Library of Congress]

Muir was a quiet, thoughtful, solitary man, more at home in the woods and mountains than in human society. Yet he was in his own way a revolutionary. His vision of nature as something to be cherished and protected—rather than consumed and exploited—was radically new in the late nineteenth and early twentieth centuries. He is America's best-known naturalist and conservationist. Muir founded the Sierra Club, has been called "the Father of the National Parks," and was a critical voice in the preservation of the Yosemite Valley, Sequoia National Park, the Grand Canyon, and other wilderness areas. He devoted his life to the protection of wild places.

The Yosemite Valley has a long history of interesting inhabitants. The Ahwahneechee Indians settled the

John Muir's "Lost Cabin," Tenaya Creek, c. 1874
[George Fiske/National Park Service, Harpers Ferry Center, Historic Photo Collection]

area several thousand years ago, living in huts known as *o-chums* at the bottom of the valley, and hunting large and small game. In the mid-1800s, the Ahwahneechee were driven out of the valley by white settlers. The son of Chief Tenaya was killed during this forced relocation, purportedly leading the chief to curse all white people who dared to set foot in Tenaya Canyon. As described in my story, Tenaya Canyon is indeed called the "Bermuda Triangle of Yosemite," and has been the site of numerous accidents and deaths due to its notoriously dangerous terrain.

The Yosemite landmarks mentioned in the book are real, but the trail that Lizzie and Tyler follow into the canyon is fictitious; hiking in Tenaya Canyon is strongly discouraged by the National Park Service.

The early white settlers of Yosemite are as described in this book. Clare Marie Hodges became the first woman park ranger in the nation, due not only to her gumption and skill on horseback but to the

Clare Marie Hodges, first woman park ranger, c. 1918
[National Park Service, Harpers Ferry Center, Historic Photo Collection]

foresight and open-mindedness of park superintendent Washington B. Lewis, who did not hesitate to hire her. Kitty Tatch and Katherine Hazelston were waitresses at the Sentinel Hotel and together became the subjects of one of the most famous early photographs of Yosemite: an image of the two women high-kicking at the edge of Glacier Point's Overhanging Rock. George Fiske, a prominent photographer of Yosemite, purportedly took this photograph as well as a photograph of John Muir's cabin. A few photographs mentioned in my story are shown here. The photograph placing Clare Hodges with Kitty Tatch in front of John

Kitty Tatch and Katherine Hazelston dancing at Overhanging Rock, Glacier Point, c.1890s
[George Fiske/National Park Service]

Muir's cabin is entirely fictitious.

And what of the lost cabin? Muir's first Yosemite cabin was a small shed built of pine, attached to the sawmill where he lived and worked from 1869 to 1871. Visitors as famous as Ralph Waldo Emerson and the botanist Asa Gray joined him there. No trace of it appears to remain, and there is confusion over its exact location. Two National Park Service plaques place it at different spots near Yosemite Falls; local legend puts it on the banks of Tenaya Creek. The cabin was almost certainly not located where Lizzie and Tyler find it in my story, but William Frederick Bade, a biographer of John Muir, wrote that Muir actually built two cabins in Yosemite, the second one near Tenaya Creek.

One of my discoveries in doing the research for this book was a funny comment by John Muir himself that refers to his "lost cabin." It appears to be a cabin he built but never lived in, on the banks of Tenaya Creek. In his *Unpublished Journals*, in a journal entry dated August 31, 1895, he writes, *"In the afternoon took a walk in search of my 'lost cabin,' as it is now*

Tenaya Canyon, as seen from Glacier Point, c. 1900s
[William Henry Jackson/Library of Congress]

called. Discovered it after a tangly search in the angle formed by Tenaya Creek with the river . . . completely hidden like a bird's nest in a charming luxuriant growth." He describes it as a structure fourteen feet by sixteen feet with a sharply sloped roof and walls that were six feet high. He writes, *"Here I longed to live in winter after being driven down from the heights by snow,"* but then notes that his plans were dashed: *"The fireplace was never built. I intended to sleep upstairs in the garret, cedar-lined and snug, and to write. The roof is mostly gone, someone has been camping in it, a bunk in a corner, a whisky bottle, cans, etc., ferns, and bushes over the floor."*

John Muir (right) with Teddy Roosevelt on Glacier Point, c.1903 [Library of Congress]

Even if John Muir never lived in the Tenaya Creek cabin, if it happened to be the shelter that Lizzie and Tyler discovered during their Yosemite adventure, I think they would have been well satisfied.

One final note: No animals were harmed in the making of this book! The plot involving the wolves is entirely fictitious. The veterinarians and zookeepers I've encountered in my life have all been singularly devoted to the health, safety, and well-being of animals, and would certainly never do anything to deliberately

make an animal sick. But for the purposes of my story, there are many substances that can produce symptoms of illness in canines temporarily, with no long-term harm. One of these is macadamia nuts, which are mildly toxic to dogs and presumably wolves, though they do not cause lasting harm or death. The symptoms of macadamia nut ingestion in canines are fever, vomiting, temporary hind limb paralysis, weakness, and muscle tremors; symptoms start within three to twelve hours and resolve without treatment in one or two days.

In my story, the zoo veterinarian uses an analgesic to sedate the wolves before transporting them to Yosemite; a likely candidate would be Domitor, which causes the animal to become unconscious but can be immediately reversed by injecting the drug Antisedan. Many, many thanks to the veterinarian Melissa Shapiro (DVM, Visiting Vet Service, Westport, Connecticut) for her medical advice; to Alex Spitzer of the Wolf Conservation Center in South Salem, New York, for his descriptions of wolf behavior; and to Jim Knox, Curator of Education at the Beardsley Zoo in Bridgeport, Connecticut, for sharing his thoughts and expertise on wolf communication and aggression, care in zoo facilities, and rehabilitation in the wild. As mentioned in my story, there are no wolves living in Yosemite currently,

 339

only coyotes. Biologists believe wolves roamed the Sierra Nevada Mountains of California several hundred years ago, but were driven to more remote areas by expanding human populations. Wolf rehabilitation efforts in our national parks have focused on Yellowstone.

ACKNOWLEDGMENTS

After the long labor of a novel, it is one of the nicest things in the world to be able to recognize the people who made it happen. I am very grateful to the following for their help in the making of this book:

My amazing editor, Christy Ottaviano, who has been the most wonderful creative partner imaginable—supportive and challenging in all the right ways—and a lovely friend, to boot.

My terrific agent, Edward Necarsulmer IV, who takes good care of the business side of things so I can focus on the artistic one.

The outstanding team at Holt, from editorial to design to marketing to sales, who work so hard behind the scenes to create beautiful books and usher them into the hands of readers.

My trio of expert advisers on wolves: Jim Knox, Curator of Education at the Beardsley Zoo in Bridgeport, Connecticut (with special thanks to my friend Bernadette Baldino, Director of the Easton Public Library and member of the Beardsley Zoo Board of Directors, for introducing me to Jim); Alex Spitzer at the Wolf Conservation Center in South Salem, New York; and Dr. Melissa Shapiro, DVM, Visiting Vet Service, Westport, Connecticut (with special thanks to my friend Susanne Smith for introducing me to Melissa).

Virginia Sanchez at the Yosemite National Park Research Library, for her help with historical photographs and interpretation.

My writer buddies, for the many conversations about plot, character, and process that have shaped my books: Nora Baskin, Ramin Ganeshram, Tommy Greenwald, Victoria Kann, Alan Katz, Bennett Madison, Natalie Standiford, Lauren Tarshis, Chris Tebbetts, Hans Wilhelm, Ellen Wittlinger, and Lisa Yee.

My fantastic readers, whose comments and reactions to drafts of my books always make them so much better: Mary Broach, Jane Burns, Claire Carlson, Laura Forte, Jane Kamensky, Carol Sheriff, Ben Daileader Sheriff,

Ellen Urheim, Zoe Wheeler, and Grace Wheeler. Additional thanks to Sophie Broach, Anna Daileader Sheriff, Jane Urheim, and Margo Urheim for conversations and brainstorming sessions that helped me along the way.

My Vermont writing retreat buddies, Jane Kamensky and Jill Lepore, who keep me connected to the world outside of children's literature and to the world of history, and whose company on dog walks through the woods has spurred many creative leaps.

And finally, an enormous thank-you to my family—Ward, Zoe, Harry, and Grace—for all they do on a daily basis to make my writing life possible.